Praise for Bhuvan Sen

"With a deft eye for detail and description, Sen offers the reader a glimpse into the lives of women who are largely ignored by society."

— MEERA EKKANATH KLEIN, AUTHOR OF THE AWARD-WINNING *MY MOTHER'S KITCHEN: A NOVEL WITH RECIPES* AND *SEEING CEREMONY*

" . . . The beauty of the stories lies in their simplicity, in which ordinary characters are able to perform heroic acts, by reaching within for strength that they themselves did not know they possessed. They are about hope and courage, grief and perseverance, and their lucidity makes them linger and endure."

— SUBHASH KAK, AUTHOR OF *THE CIRCLE OF MEMORY* AND *ARRIVAL AND EXILE*

MY WAR, MY CHILD

Copyright © 2024 by Bharati Sen

All cover art copyright © 2024

paperback ISBN: 9781955836210

eBook ISBN: 9781955836203

hardcover ISBN: 9781955836227

My War, My Child

BHARATI SEN

ADMISSION PRESS

For all the women and children hurt by war.

Acknowledgments

There's nothing quite like the feeling of someone believing in you. You would not be reading this book without the continued support and vision of my editor and publisher, Lara Bernhardt, who has displayed her enormous skill and precision in guiding this story into shape. Her words of encouragement and her tenacity have been invaluable to me. I could not have made it this far without her.

My writing life would not have been possible without the support of many people, whom I'd like to acknowledge and thank. First, I'd like to thank my family for their unwavering belief in me. Also, to my son for giving a fitting title to my story. I thank my dearest friends for appreciating everything I've written.

I'd also like to thank you, my cherished readers. I am happy that I can share my story with the world.

MY WAR
MY CHILD

BHARATI SEN

WWW.ADMISSIONPRESS.COM

"Women have always been the primary victims of war. Women lose their husbands, their fathers, their sons in combat. Women often have to flee from the only homes they have ever known. Women are often the refugees from conflict and sometimes, more frequently, in today's warfare, victims. Women are often left with the responsibility, alone, of raising the children."

— HILARY CLINTON

One

THE FAIRGROUND

Afsana slowed her pace and smiled at her six-year-old daughter, Razia. The little girl walked fast, almost running, and her hair fluttered in the breeze as she tried to keep up with her mother's quick pace and longer strides. When she nearly tripped, Afsana caught her hand and squeezed it.

Razia ran her fingers over the glass bangles her mother wore, causing them to clatter and clink. Afsana loved her daughter's excitement, which reminded her of her own childhood thrill at fairs and celebrations. Happier times.

The sun blazed down on them, creating a haziness that rendered everything fuzzy. Light, frothy clouds, high in the sky, offered no shade. Afsana raised one hand to her forehead to block the sun's harsh glare. The hot wind pelted them with gritty dust and sand, kicked up from hurried footsteps of the crowd and by the eddies of wind whirling around the field.

Taking in hand a small handkerchief she always kept hidden in her bosom, Afsana wiped the dirt from her daughter's face. She, too, tasted the grit in her mouth.

"Razia, my jewel, hold my hand and stay close. I don't want us to lose each other in the crowds."

"Yes, Ammu. I'll stay close," she said.

"Look at this unruly crowd. They'll push you away from me, and I will not know where to find you." Afsana placed a protective hand on her shoulder, and the girl snuggled close.

It was April 14th, and the fair at Ranaghat in West Bengal, India was kicking off on schedule, a welcome excitement for Afsana and the entire community to celebrate the traditional Bengali New Year, otherwise known as *Poila Boishakh*. Rides and stalls were already up. The enormous fairground bustled with activity, crowded with people of all ages, jostling and elbowing each other in breathless excitement.

Traditionally, businesses would start on this auspicious day with a new ledger. Families would visit relatives in brand-new outfits, eat sumptuous meals, and indulge in a variety of sweets to complete the celebration. They would let go of the past year and welcome the new one. Afsana and Razia did not have extended family to visit, so the fair was their highlight of the holiday.

The month-long fair with its sprawling, outdoor stalls serving all varieties of food allowed them to enjoy the forgotten recipes of traditional Bengali cuisine. Despite the overwhelming stale smell of reheated and reused oil pervading the air, people lined up for hot sizzling eggplant and onion fritters, *samosas*, crispy *pakoras*, all fried in batches in gigantic cauldrons. The mouthwatering scent of *kachoris*, served with hot gram and potato curry, reached the nose before the food reached the mouth. Cotton candies in plastic bags and sugar sticks were an added treat for the children. The longest lines were found at the stalls selling the exquisite stars of Bengali sweets—hot *jalebis*, colorful *barfis*, *gulab jamuns*, and *rasgullas*.

If the food scene wasn't impressive enough, the skilled artisans of West Bengal displayed their equally impressive talent throughout the fairgrounds. Afsana always looked forward to the entertainment, with singers and dancers staging *jatra*—traditional plays. Stalls displayed terracotta wall plaques with unique designs, carefully carved utensils, dolls, and colorful animals stacked on tables. She knew these artisans tried to make the most out of these fairs, which could be a big bonus to their meager income during the remainder of the year. She watched with a discerning eye to decide what she would carry to her home.

Ropewalkers and magicians performed. A juggler showed off his tricks. Razia shrunk against her as they passed a snake charmer playing a tune on his flute in front of a king cobra, which bobbed back and forth with its hood raised. A large and enthusiastic crowd gathered to cheer, but when the show was over, only a few dropped coins on the piece of cloth laid out on the ground for contributions.

As an only child, Razia did not meet too many people, and Afsana could tell the crowded fair fascinated her. After spending some time sampling different stalls, Razia noticed a great rush of girls her age at a small stall selling items like *bindis*, hair clips, headbands, and an array of glass bangles arranged in glittering rainbow colors hanging down in spirals around bamboo poles. Razia lingered at the stall, admiring all the unique styles, cuts, and sparkling colors. She touched them gingerly.

"Can I buy the green ones, Ammu?" Razia tugged at her mother's arm.

"Why green?" Afsana asked. "There are so many other colorful ones. Why not the red with gold dots?" She sifted through the many stacks of bangles stringed together.

"No, the green ones will match the color of my slippers," Razia insisted.

The fairgrounds reminded Afsana of her own younger days. The food at these fairs tasted especially good. She knew it was not only the hands that prepared them, but that the place itself was a taste of time, as if the blistering heat, the clamoring crowds, the dust, the light-hearted banter of the people, and the loud music all came together to paint the perfect picture of her own childhood and flavor the moment.

4 · BHARATI SEN

The smell of food broke through her thoughts. Afsana stepped into the crowd, led by the enticing smells, pushing her way to a vendor who was frying mouth-watering eggplant fritters in a large cauldron.

"Let's eat and look around first. We can always come back," she said.

The eggplant fritters tasted every bit as good as Afsana had expected. She walked on light feet, continuing to take in the sights.

As little children gathered around to ride the merry-go-round, Razia was mesmerized by the up and down movement of the wooden horses of the carousel. She looked in awe at the seats rotating in synchrony to the accompaniment of music. When she saw a little boy of three or four whining to go for a ride, she gave her mother a gentle nudge and an expectant look.

Afsana smiled upon her with approval and helped her find an empty seat, lifting her gently onto the saddle of the wooden horse. As the giant wheel began to rotate, Razia turned and waved at her mother, whose loving eyes were fixed on her daughter's face.

For a moment, Afsana became quiet and rather reflective, caught in her own thoughts with a dull ache of realization. *How beautiful my daughter is. I pray she resembles me more than her father. Perhaps one day I can tell her the truth. But for the time being, Razia doesn't have to know.*

That would be the hardest part, seeking the understanding of her daughter. An observant eye could see by her apparent sadness that there was a weak spot in her heart, a memory of what happened, that Afsana wanted to erase forever. Her husband, Shiraj, had proven himself to be a good father, and Razia meant more to him than anything else in the world. He made it known repeatedly to his Afsana that nothing whatsoever should come between them. Both had gone through difficult times and had found solace in each other.

Afsana thought back to some of her childhood memories,

happier times before life had battered her. She remembered things that she had not thought about for many years. She'd grown up in the city of Dhaka and missed the grand style in which *Pohela Boishakh* was celebrated when she was younger. Back then, the holiday began by first scrubbing and cleaning everything. Afsana remembered fondly how she adorned herself with flowers and bangles and draped herself in a white saree with a red border for the ceremony welcoming the New Year. At home, her mother always made the traditional breakfast of *panta bhat*, a rice-based dish prepared by soaking cooked rice overnight, traditionally served with fried fish, green chilies, onion, and pickles.

She missed her parents deeply. She had not seen her mother in so long. And the last time she saw her father—

Razia signaled her mother, asking for help getting down from the merry-go-round.

"Did you have fun?" Afsana asked.

Razia's beaming face said it all. As the two continued to stroll down the packed walkways, it slowly dawned on Afsana that there was something unusual about this day. The air buzzed with energy, imparting a sense of wonder, a sense of something more. The smell, the sultry air, the shouts of hawkers, and the fair itself seemed different this year. All around her she felt the presence of heavenly melodies sung by ethereal voices. All this was so extraordinary, so unexpected, so bewildering, she was altogether like a person in a trance.

Transfixed, lost in thought, Afsana didn't realize she'd lost Razia until she turned around and the girl was gone. Afsana jolted back to reality and frantically scanned the crowds. Tears welled up in her eyes as she thought of the worst possibilities. She called out Razia's name over and over into the open crowd, a churning sea of people that had swallowed her daughter. Fear continued to consume her. Had she been kidnapped? Did she wander off somewhere? Agonizing minutes passed, but still there was no sign of her.

An eternity seemed to pass as Afsana twisted this way and that, searching, losing hope. And then she caught a glimpse of a little girl. She stood stock-still and took a deep breath of relief as she recognized the familiar face. But her daughter was not alone. A man—a stranger—was striding along with the girl, guiding her through the crowd with a gentle hand on one elbow.

"There you are!" Afsana rushed toward her daughter and cradled her in her arms. "Razia, my jewel, I've been looking everywhere for you!" she gushed, straining to catch her breath as she snuggled against her daughter's soft, warm neck, shedding bitter tears.

Afsana gazed at the stranger and smiled. "You've been most kind. I don't know how to thank you enough. Razia is my only child, my whole world, and I'm so grateful to you for finding her for me."

"Your little one wandered to my bangle stall," the man said. "I promised to help find her Ammu. I merely helped her to find the place where she was separated from you."

Afsana's heart skipped as she heard the man's voice. Still crouched down with Razia in her arms, she stared up at the man, speechless. That voice. She knew that voice.

The stranger gave a half-smile and nodded his head before quickly turning away and, in an instant, disappearing amongst the influx of people.

He gave no indication he recognized her as she recognized him. *Has it really been that long?* Six years and yet an entire lifetime it seemed. From the gray ruins of memory, the sound of his voice brought back recollections of her buried past—the memories she thought she had put away forever.

Could he be the man she believed him to be?

The man she believed was long gone.

Her first husband, taken from her much too soon.

Two

THE OWNER OF THE GLASS BANGLE STALL

Afsana resolutely tried to thrust her thoughts aside as she and Razia made their way home, but those recurring thoughts could not be evaded—they returned again and again with overwhelming force. When she arrived home, she stared at Shiraj. Her flustered state must have been clear on her face.

"You are shivering, Afsana. I hope you have not caught an infection." Her husband touched the hand she extended, worry lines creasing his forehead.

"It will pass," she said and hoped it was true.

The next day, the man from the glass bangle stall crept back to her memory, unwilling to leave her in peace. He couldn't be the man from her past she had mistaken him to be.

Could he?

He couldn't.

"I shall forget," she tried to convince herself, but the brief encounter could not be so easily dismissed, replaying over and over in her mind with utmost vividness. Uneasiness grew within her as she recollected the shape of his hands, which held her daughter's. Those beautiful, long, tapered fingers had fine lines of scars. She had not failed to notice the thin but discernible marks of old wounds on his face. The most prominent one was the large scar that ran diagonally from under his left ear down to his chin, preventing hair from growing, leaving a silvery pinkish line through his disheveled beard.

And yet, those scars did not detract at all from the natural handsomeness of his face. One could tell that each mark on his body had a story to tell. His piercing eyes seemed to haunt her again and again.

Afsana, impelled by a wild hope, set out to the fairground the following morning. Instead of entering the glass bangle stall, she stationed herself at the sweets stall that commanded a view of the man selling bangles. She could not have selected a better spot, calculated for the purpose of having a clear view of the man, observing him without being seen.

Soon, she came out of her hiding place and entered the bangle stall, determined to solve the mystery once and for all. Her heart thumped, both from nervousness and at the pleasure of seeing him again. Despite the carnival around her—the throngs of happy people, the music, the shouts of vendors—a thousand expectations arose and confronted her and all her strength of will failed to steady her trembling hands.

He did not look up when she came in. She watched him carefully, afraid she was mistaken, but more afraid her suspicions were correct.

"Have you been here for a long time?" His eyes remained fixed on stacking the glass bangles and tying them with ribbon. Would he never look at her?

"No, not at all. I just came along."

"Did you come to get more bangles for your daughter? I have some new ones that she might like."

"That's very kind of you," she said, smiling at him. "I'll bring her tomorrow. I'm sure she'll love them." She paused for a moment. "You remind me of someone I used to know."

"Is that so?"

"I have lost touch with him for many years, but he was very dear to me. His name was Farzad."

The man looked up and appeared to be in deep thought, staring off into space. Afsana held her breath. But then he shook his head. "I'm sorry. I do not know anybody by that name."

She came closer and looked directly at him, longing for recognition to light his eyes. "You don't recognize me? It's me, Afsana."

His head bent slightly and when he looked up this time, he stared directly back at her. But his blank eyes remained empty. Afsana had been through countless misfortunes in her life. She had confronted them and overcome her troubles, but for the first time in a very long time, she felt helpless, watching the face of the man who seemed so familiar to her. And yet saw her as a complete stranger.

Grief and bitterness filled her heart. Every look, every gesture, came alive in her mind, as if it was yesterday. As her heart raced, she knew the years had not diminished her love for him.

She dared not utter a word that might unsettle him, and if she felt any surprise at his changed looks, she did not betray her disappointment. She could only watch his eyes, now dull and devoid of luster. The eyes that once captivated her heart were furtive, timid. Those eyes that she never expected to see again.

With a glance at the setting sun, she bid him goodbye.

"Remember to bring your little girl tomorrow," he reminded her.

"Of course. See you tomorrow."

Tears welled in her eyes once again as she turned away, her heart sick within her. A cold chill seemed to pass over her, killing all her hopes.

Farzad, my first love, where were you all these years? Where have I not looked for you? Why can't you remember me? Her thoughts rumbled over her like an avalanche of sorrows.

Afsana realized she had continued to live wrapped up in the

memory of her lost husband, harboring a secret hope he would someday return. Everything else mattered less to her. And now, his unexpected return to her life stirred up a deep yearning for this man from her past.

The agony and the ecstasy of seeing him brought about a raging storm in her heart. She had thought him dead and had made her peace with that. She had come to terms with her new life years ago. Had she not harbored feelings for Farzad, had she not waited for this moment, everything would have been just as it was. Now that he had returned, how could her life continue on the same?

And yet how could it change? She was married to another man, and Farzad seemed not to remember her. She had no choice but to struggle against the weaknesses of her feelings and to fulfill her duties as a wife to Shiraj.

As promised, the next morning Afsana returned and brought Razia with her. While they were at the stall browsing, she thought she saw a momentary spark of recognition in his eyes. But perhaps it was only her imagination showing her what she wanted to see. Or delight in returning customers.

"It is nice to see you both again," he greeted them at the front of the stall. He took out a bunch of colorful bangles from his large pockets.

"These are durable bangles specially made for little girls. They don't break easily." He put the sets of bangles into Razia's eager hands.

"How much do I owe you?" Afsana asked.

"Oh no, nothing. I brought these bangles for Razia." He brushed aside her thanks and after some hesitation casually remarked, "She looks just like you."

"Yes, she does. She does look like me." Afsana ruffled Razia's silky black hair and admired her big brown eyes, gently brushing back an errant strand of hair from her thick, arched eyebrows. How fortunate that when she looked at her daughter, her own features were reflected back and not those of her father, a constant reminder of the loss—

The pain of the moment was almost too much to bear.

His forehead creased as he seemed to register the look on her face before she could hide it. She noticed a flute in his pocket and gestured to it.

"Do you play the flute?" Afsana asked, her voice bright with astonishment. She smoothed her frown and forced a smile in its place.

A shadow crossed Farzad's face, hinting at deepest darkness. He took a minute to answer. Afsana could sense he was reluctant to talk about it.

"Not so much, but someday I hope to play like I used to. Sometimes I feel as though I have played it for a long time, and the melodies that I play are all known tunes. Those tunes, they come easily," he answered, fumbling for the flute that bulged out from one of the large pockets of his loose shirt.

"Where did you learn to play? I knew someone a long time back who played the flute," she said.

"I don't remember exactly how I learned, but when I play it, images from the distant past come back. But they are all disconnected and hazy," he replied.

A pale, wintry smile flickered for an instant across his face, the glimmer of a half-memory beneath his blank forgetfulness. Years ago, it had been a smile full of sunlight and dear to her heart. Farzad had frequently played his flute to his beloved Afsana, moments she'd taken for granted but now pined for.

"I am certain you play beautifully." Afsana flushed a little.

Farzad's gaze intensified. "I can't explain it, but you feel so familiar to me, like we have always known each other. Who are you? Have I known you before?"

"I—"

He stepped closer as if enchanted by her. "Who are you that seems so much mine, yet not mine?"

"Farzad," she said gently. She trembled a little, and her eyes became moist. "Look at me and try to remember our college days. We spent so much time together. Can't you remember? The Liberation Movement? Our days at Dhaka University? In between writing slogans and our clandestine meetings with the other comrades, you played the flute sitting near the bank of the river. Remember us sitting beneath the banyan tree?"

He gave her an intense look, but his features remained unchanged. "I have seen you somewhere I think, perhaps in the old times before I came here. But my memory is poor, very poor. What is your name again?"

"Afsana," she answered, willing the word to act like a spell, to break the curse and unlock his lost memories.

"Afsana?" he repeated in an impassioned voice. "It is a sweet name. I feel as if I knew somebody by that name but as I said, I have forgotten many things."

Her heart pounded violently against her chest with a mix of doubt and expectation as she willed him with all her might to remember.

"Afsana," he repeated once again, eyes closed, as if casting his net as far and as wide as possible in the river of memories, trying to snare any recollection, anything at all from his life, anything that even distantly resembled the name Afsana.

His face lit up and a wave of pleasure seemed to sweep over him. She dared to hope that her presence had worked magic on him, reconnecting him with the time when their lives had entwined so deeply and yet which he had so mysteriously forgotten.

"It is faint," he finally said. "Very faint. But I think I do remember something. And you, Afsana. I am glad to see you once again."

"And I you," Afsana replied with a faint smile. "What can you remember?"

"Little. Only shadows lost in a depth I cannot seem to raise them from. What can you tell me that might help?" he asked, his eyes pleading with mournful simplicity.

"Where have you been, Farzad? What happened to you?"

The dove gray sky of the evening had now crept all over the fairground, announcing the coming sunset. Although it was a true summer evening, with the sun gradually disappearing over the horizon, everything was calm and softly tinted. And the sky seemed to know every one of his thoughts, his dreams, his darkest fears. His face glowed with the last orange rays and his lips bore the semblance of a smile, just enough to show that he was enjoying his thoughts, whatever they may be.

"I have a brother," he said all of a sudden. "Did you know him? What can you tell me about him?"

"Your brother Alam was a valiant soldier, " Afsana answered, her voice trailing off.

"But you don't mean—you surely cannot mean that poor Alam is no more. Is my brother dead?" As she spoke, a dark sadness crept over her listener's face.

"He is," she said, devastated that he must hear the news from her all over again.

His face darkened. "I had forgotten we had so much sorrow in our youth."

"We did." She had the benefit of years to distance herself from the pain of those memories. Farzad had been jolted back to them, fresh and startling.

"And you, Afsana. What about yourself?"

Afsana looked down at her feet, not knowing how to tell him about herself.

"Oh, Farzad, I am Shiraj's wife now."

"What do you mean?" he asked her. "Who is Shiraj?"

Suddenly she saw the folly of her intent to bring this man back to her. What could come of it but more sorrow?

"Farzad, I did not know you were alive. You never came back to me after the night we parted. I should have waited for you but

— So many things happened. I still do not understand. It looks like you have been very ill for a long time. Years have passed without you knowing it. Where have you been?"

"Years? How long?" he asked in a low whisper.

"About six years."

"Six years!"

"I am so sorry, Farzad."

"I cannot understand it yet, and it will take a while for me to understand everything, but it brings a lot of solace to me knowing that while so much is lost, you are still here, and you are still the same," he told her.

"For me too, Farzad. I am so glad to know you are alive."

Razia tugged at her sleeve. "Ammu, when can we leave?"

She had forgotten all about her daughter, so lost in the past she had forgotten her present. A present that included a daughter and another man who was now her husband. "I must go, Farzad."

"Already? I have only begun to remember."

"I need to take Razia home. But I hope to see you again."

"I hope for that too." He lifted his hand.

"I love the bangles," Razia said.

"Yes, thank you." Afsana had forgotten the reason for their visit completely. She turned to leave, grief squeezing her heart as she walked away from her first love.

Three

CONFLICTING PASSIONS

After a month or so, the holiday ended. The vendors at the fair dispersed as quickly as they had gathered as the fair was coming to an end. In order to help increase their profits, they used discount pricing to attract price-sensitive customers, and exclusive deals on favorite items were common practice at these fairs.

"Can we go to the fair before the stalls are gone? I want to buy more bangle sets to match my other outfits," Razia told her mother.

Afsana stood up abruptly, as if her daughter could read her mind. She had been restless the whole day. And there were now those familiar stirrings inside her, desperation to meet Farzad again clouding her every moment. Time to see him again was limited.

Thus, in the pitiless afternoon sun, both mother and daughter took the familiar road to the fair. As the events at the fair were ending, there were fewer people on the road. The vast sheet of open ground stretched endlessly in front of them.

A gentle, warm breeze swept over the field, bringing some relief to the wanderers. And to their dismay, they found that many vendors had already closed their stalls—and one of them was the glass bangle stall. No trace remained except for the stake holes.

Afsana went on looking for Farzad. She approached one of the other vendors, hoping to get some information regarding him but was disappointed at their nonchalant answers.

She stood motionless, absorbed in her thoughts. A hopeless sigh escaped her lips. Clenching her hands and pressing them hard against her forehead, Afsana whispered, "You've left me again." She hastily wiped tears from her face with the free end of her saree, and when there were no more tears to shed, she took hold of her daughter's hand.

"Let's go home, Razia. He's gone."

"Who's gone?" Razia looked puzzled at her mother.

"The man who gave you the bangles," she answered. "I wanted to see him once more, but I suppose we shall never meet again. I came here so that he may know how much I am going to miss him."

"Will he come back next year? How am I going to get bangles?" Razia asked.

"I don't know," Afsana replied, not wanting to talk anymore.

"Ammu, maybe he'll come back with more bangles. Let's go home now."

Her daughter's sweet voice, full of concern, reminded her of what was most important and soothed the aching of her heart.

As they were about to leave the fairground, something caught her eye. She crouched low, thrust her bare arm inside one of the holes of the stakes where the something lay half submerged. She took it out, turned it over and examined it with trembling hands, then pressed it against her chest with exquisite sadness. It was Farzad's flute wrapped in a scarf. Afsana tried hard to hold back her sobs, but Razia saw tears brimming in her eyes. She ran over to her mother and put her small arm around her.

"Why are you crying, Ammu? Have you hurt yourself? Don't cry, Ammu!" Razia stroked her hair.

"No, my sweet, don't you see? I am smiling too." Afsana was still distraught, but she forced herself to smile at Razia's kind words. "I don't know what it is, but it is so quiet here that it brings tears to my eyes. Why don't you walk by my side and hold my hand? It will make me a lot happier."

Razia strode along next to her mother, and it was indeed a pleasure to hear the pit-pat of dainty, smart stepping of her little slippers on the hard soil of the ground.

The flute brought some solace, a vague hope that he might come back to retrieve it. She still wondered why Farzad's face did not light up when he first saw her. His inability to show any sign of recognition confused her. He must have gone through a traumatic event, a dangerous experience that could have a long-term impact on his body as well as on his mind. What had happened during his absence from her life, those lost years? Perhaps she would never know.

Several months later, as Afsana served breakfast to Shiraj, she happened to glance at the local Bengali newspaper he was reading.

A small article caught her attention. It was about the Bangladesh Liberation Movement of 1971 and the role played by the *Mukti Bahini,* the Bangladesh Forces. The newspaper mentioned the name of a particular *Mukti Joddha,* a freedom fighter, who had returned to Dhaka after several years. A freedom fighter by the name of Farzad Mansour.

She stopped in her tracks. Farzad had returned to Dhaka. Was that because she had spoken to him about their time at Dhaka University? Dhaka was a big city but at least she knew his general whereabouts. Her immediate and visceral reaction to this news confirmed that she still had feelings for Farzad. She wondered how Shiraj would react if she set out to find her first husband.

Pouring out the tea, she handed a cup to Shiraj, sugared it to his taste, and then prepared one for herself. Shiraj ate silently, quite intent upon his breakfast, every now and then glancing at the newspaper, which lay by his plate.

He gulped down another cup of tea, pushed away his cup and saucer, and fell back in his chair. He flipped through the pages of the newspaper. There was no way he could have missed the article. She wondered if he had seen it or if she could casually draw his attention to it. But he decided for her.

"Could it be possible that this Farzad, whose name I see in the article, was your former husband? The newspaper mentioned only the names of war heroes who survived the war with the purpose of rewarding them."

"Do you think it could be him?" Her voice sounded strange, a strained, high-pitched tone announcing her anxiety.

"Why, Afsana, you seem edgy."

"Well, if this is him, then my first husband is still alive." The whispered words hung in the air as her second husband digested them.

"Do you still care about him?" Shiraj's voice held a tone of reserve. Afsana kept quiet. She had been waiting for an opportunity to talk about her encounter with Farzad. Now she regretted that she never had.

"I have something to tell you Shiraj—something that I have been struggling to say for months, and I don't know how to."

Shiraj only stared, as if trying to read the minutest detail of her face to see if he should be concerned.

"Remember when Razia and I visited the fairgrounds a few months back and bought glass bangles? And we went again and again? I returned not just to buy the bangles but also to see the owner of the glass bangle stall. I wanted to tell you what happened at the fair. But I went there without you knowing anything about it and didn't know how to say it. To my amazement, I found out that the man at the shop was no other than Farzad."

"He survived the war?" Shiraj's face expressed first delight, then shock at what this meant. "You saw him and talked to him? And you didn't tell me anything about it?"

She hung her head, unable to look at him. "I wanted to, Shiraj. It is just such a difficult thing."

"How can you be sure?" her husband asked in a tone of disbelief. Then he shook his head. "He was killed in the war many years ago. This was probably simply a man who resembled him."

"It was him, Shiraj, even though one could hardly recognize him, for he had changed a lot. I knew he was my husband. His face bore all the marks of pain and torture that he must have endured during the war. His eyes were restless and there was a long deep scar on his face. He did not even recognize me." She went to a cupboard and brought out the hidden instrument. "But he left this. His flute."

He uncrossed his legs and slid forward toward Afsana, taking the flute gently in his hands. "I know this flute."

"How can that be?"

"It was so long ago, I had nearly forgotten. Surely, I did treat a man who was in very bad shape with severe cuts and wounds all over his face. When he was brought to the hospital, he didn't know his name or how old he was, if his family were alive or dead, from where he came, or his whereabouts. I still remember the blank looks when he was interrogated. His traumatic brain injury left him with significant memory loss. When I realized the extent of his amnesia, I referred him to an eminent neuropsychologist, but he disappeared and there was no trace of him after that."

"And you think that was Farzad?"

Shiraj turned toward his wife. "The patient retained some of his motor skills. It was as if time stopped for him ever since he had that injury. This is the same flute a little boy gave him while he was at the hospital."

"Why would a little boy give him the flute?" she asked.

"The boy was a patient at the hospital. He had been hit by

shrapnel from a bomb. While he was recuperating, his father brought a flute thinking that it might keep him occupied and help him forget his pain. The little boy knew how to play. The amnesiac patient next to his bed sprang forward, reaching for the instrument. The flute came to life at the vibrant touch of his fingers. Although his memory failed him, the man had not forgotten how to play the flute. The boy's father gifted the flute to him when his son was released and left the hospital, fully recovered. Soon the man who played the flute so well made friends with the whole hospital staff, entertaining them with his music."

"You treated my missing husband before we even met. And yet you had no idea."

"The world is a strange place. We never learned his name. But this is wonderful! Farzad fought for our country valiantly. I am delighted to learn he survived, even if he is not the same man you remember."

She knew Shiraj's delight at the discovery of Farzad's survival was sincere and strong, knowing that Farzad fought heroically for the freedom and liberation of the country. But if he could look into his wife's heart, he would not be elated over the reappearance of her first husband, for Afsana's heart panted at the idea of reconnecting with him.

"Shiraj, please, can you help me find him?" she said.

"And how would we set about to do that? I have no information to start from. How can you find a person in the big city of Dhaka? And I don't think it would be proper for you to meet up with him. You told me Farzad didn't remember you."

"No, that's not true. He did remember me eventually. At least, he slowly regained some memories."

"And what about Razia? She knows me as her father. You don't want to uproot her from where she belongs."

"You are thinking way too far ahead. I'm not going anywhere. All I want is to find him, to know what happened to him, his whereabouts during those years when we were separated."

"And how do you expect to know, when that part of his life is completely wiped out from his memory?"

"Perhaps I can help him to remember. And wouldn't that be better for him than suffering a gaping hole in his life?"

Afsana knew that she was still attached to Farzad emotionally and part of her longed to get back to the lost days when they were together. For she loved the nature and reliability of her present husband but craved the rebelliousness and passion of her first husband. But she convinced herself that this was for Farzad's good. It would be right to go and meet up with him if there was any chance she could help him. She tried to ignore how much her heart rejoiced at the thought of seeing him again.

Shiraj grappled with something he'd never felt before—jealousy. Whatever secret regrets and disappointments he had indulged upon in the solitude of his own soul, the thought of a prior attachment had never crossed his mind—and he did not suffer the agonies of jealousy till the realization he was married to another man's wife. And that man had prior claims to the woman he loved. After a period of shock and disbelief, Shiraj slowly began to comprehend the whole situation.

A few days after this new revelation, he woke up with the thought that Afsana was not overjoyed to see him. She went about life as normal, but he watched her intently for some sign that she adored him as he adored her—and he saw no evidence of this. His heart began to ache in an unfamiliar way.

She would occasionally mention Farzad in casual conversations, but Shiraj began to read subtext into her words. He convinced himself Afsana no longer loved him and perhaps never had.

Every time I look at you, I am entranced by your beautiful eyes. But every time I look at you, your face says something else—that you are never thinking about me.

Still, he carried on as normal. Until one evening when he returned home after work. Something wasn't right. As he approached the house, his eyes sought the windows as always, but no one watched for him. Little Razia normally stood resolutely, waiting for him to return from work. Her face lighting up at the sight of him was always a highlight of his days.

The locked door further confounded him. Had they all forgotten the time of day? He rapped three times, trying not to imagine horrible things that kept his wife and daughter from their usual places. But Afsana did not greet him. The maid opened the door. As he stepped inside the house, one of his first impulses was to shout for Razia at the foot of the stairs.

The silence struck him with an odd feeling. There was no distracting sound from anywhere in the entire house—everything was exceptionally quiet, and his mind began to uneasily churn with conjecture.

"What's up?" he exclaimed. "Where is everybody?"

"They are not at home. They left this afternoon," the maid replied.

"What's all this mystery? Tell me and be quick with it."

"It is not my place to interfere," she answered and scurried to her room.

He sat down heavily as if overcome by fatigue. A faintness of spirit slowly seized him as he covered his face with his hands.

He felt worn and aged within this short span of time. When he laughed, it was a mirthless hollow laugh. He went into his study, lit a small lamp, and spotted a note on the table. He picked it up and began to read it, a stone of worry growing in his stomach.

Dear Shiraj,

I know this will take you off guard, but I need some time away from Calcutta. You know how

I feel about Farzad or at least felt at one point in my life. His resurrection has brought back to life the unanswered questions I had buried and said farewell to years ago. I need answers, closure for which I need to go back to Dhaka. You have given me the greatest possible happiness and my heart shatters as I write this letter. Please take care of yourself. I am taking Razia with me, even though I know this will cause an additional source of worry. I have no choice. Please try to understand.

Love,

Afsana

He read the note thrice over, balled up the paper in his hand, crumpling it until it was a tiny ball before he tossed it away. He sat back and sighed. After a while, he went to Razia's bedroom, and a cold chill of fear swept through him. Anyone looking at his determined face would have said there was a spasm of jealous anger there—but it was anger against his own person.

How I wish she told me of her intentions to go to Dhaka. She has not been fair to me. His swollen heart heaved with anger. She snuck off while he was at work, only letting him know her decision—something as significant as this!—through a little chit of paper. And only after she had acted on it. He had never stopped her from living her life, and he did not ever intend to, but this was unlike anything he had ever imagined.

He had built his life around Afsana and Razia. And now Farzad returned and could take it all away? The idea of never again returning home to his daughter's smiling face, of an empty house, an empty bed, made him sick with worry.

At the same time, he felt disgruntled for not being able to

blame Afsana entirely for the goings-on. How was she to know that Farzad, her supposedly long-dead husband, would re-emerge from the past? How was she to know that Farzad's return to her life would disturb the fine balance of matrimony that they both had so lovingly and tenderly built? He would fight for his family and his life, although a confrontation with Farzad was not exactly what he was looking for at this moment. How was he, Shiraj, to know that when he pledged to care for Afsana, she was not truly free to marry?

He could still recall her first words all those years ago, and the tenderness of her voice, how every vein in his body went rapturous when he saw the gleam of her shining eyes. It was then he realized that he wanted to spend the rest of his life by her side. Now, it seemed it was all over, that she for whom his soul restlessly burned could be another's. With a sinking heart, he waited anxiously for her return.

Four

THE HEARTBREAKER

Walking through the old Dhaka streets, Afsana felt exuberant. This was her first visit since she left the city in 1971, when the liberation war was raging on. She hired a cycle rickshaw and, on a whim, visited the home where she grew up. She spent the whole morning roaming around the empty house and in the afternoon sat under the enormous plantain tree which covered and shaded the entire area. *I still love this place and I am still so attached to it by my deep roots.*

"This is where I lived when I was your age," she told Razia.

"Where are your Ammu and Abbu?" Razia asked in her innocent way.

Fresh pain tugged at Afsana's heart, for she considered them lost in the war, as she had considered Farzad long gone. What if, like Farzad, her parents had survived? Could she someday stumble across them too? And yet, if they lived, surely they would have returned to this house, their only home. The fact that it remained empty and desolate, six years of decay evident, told her the painful truth.

"I lost them years ago, my jewel." She pulled Razia close. "How I wish they could have met you."

She planned to meet up with Farzad at Ahsan Manjil, a prominent tourist spot, situated near the river. *What a delicious morning it is*, she thought, as she stared at the Buriganga River, a tide-influenced river which passed south and west of Dhaka city. Launches and ferry boats provided a connection to the other parts of Bangladesh.

Her pulse raced, the blood rushing with an exulting thrill in Afsana's small frame, when she met Farzad. She nearly threw her arms about him in a hug but stopped short.

"Farzad," she said, searching his face for clues as to his feelings for her. "I've come to see you."

His eyes searched her face in return. She saw clarity in them and recognition and realized that Farzad must have regained all of his memories after he came back to Dhaka—but made no effort to contact her. And she began to feel extremely uneasy next to this man who once was so familiar, so much a part of her life. And yet with whom after those momentous years apart, she felt unacquainted.

He leaned closer and whispered, "What are you doing in Dhaka? You shouldn't be here, Afsana. I want you to go back to Calcutta. There's nothing left here for you. What we had, what we fought for, doesn't exist anymore."

"Are you not happy to see me?"

Instead of answering, he tousled Razia's hair. "Shall we walk to the park?"

She saw how decidedly uncomfortable he looked, as if, were he offered any option to escape at this very moment, he would not have hesitated to do so. Perhaps he remembered that a soldier must never run away from any situation. They walked on in silence, listening to the sound of their own steps, and presently she felt a freshness in the air coming from the riverfront. He walked so quickly, she was incapable of keeping in step with Farzad. *Why isn't he speaking to me,* she thought.

They crossed the road in order to reach the railing along the river, and there they stood, sending Razia to play in the park.

Cold air blew up from the water, and Afsana wrapped her shawl snuggly about herself. They found a tree to lean against. Farzad too stared into the water. Then he moved closer to the railing and put one of his feet against the iron bar.

"Do you remember the banyan tree at Dhaka University?" she asked, hoping to prompt a happy memory. "I considered it our tree."

"I could be wrong, but I think I remember hearing it was cut down when Pakistani forces invaded."

Cut down, like her marriage to Farzad, leaving a stump where it should have thrived. "It was at that."

He turned to her. "You are married to another man, Afsana. Have given him a beautiful daughter. What we had is nothing but a dream. Only an unfulfilled dream."

"But you promised me that nothing would change. You promised you would come back to me. Look at me—I have not changed. And now we have been reunited by chance, I can't believe—"

"Of course you have changed. Those years changed everything."

"If only you could remember—"

"I remember everything. It has all come back to me. I remember sitting on this bench near the river in the evenings, pulling up my legs, leaning my head against the wooden back of the bench to stare at you. And sometimes playing my flute softly and watching the cloudless skies."

She believed that the man who had unquestionably loved her once must love her still, that he was incapable of change. But who was this man who looked at her with veiled eyes and spoke in a voice she did not know and bore little resemblance to the one who once wrapped her in his loving arms and had thrilled her with the rapture of his kisses?

"If you remember all that, how can you be so cold to me? You will just forget about us?"

"Afsana, I'll always love you, but I can't take you back. You have a loving husband now and an adorable daughter. I have nothing to offer you."

"I still love you. My heart still aches for you."

"But to what end? We cannot be together now. Please go."

"At least tell me what happened to you. Where have you been? You promised nothing would stop you from coming back to me, but you never did. Why? I deserve to know."

"What happened to me?" Farzad produced a gruff sound, something between a laugh and a cough. "A series of misfortunes struck me one after another, so relentlessly that it seemed fate plotted against me."

Lifting her eyes to her first husband's face, she whispered, "Then tell me, Farzad. Tell me about those lost years, and how you survived when everyone believed you had died at the hands of our enemies."

Spreading his handkerchief over the worn wooden bench, he asked her to be seated.

"We suffered a major setback owing to the enemy's strong reinforcements. Have you heard about the Monsoon Offensive? How could you, you probably didn't even see the daylight at the military camps."

"Farzad, I know about the Monsoon Offensive, everyone was affected by the outcome," Afsana replied.

"We chose the rainy season because we calculated that Pakistani soldiers, not having any experience with the monsoons and the heavy rain, would be an easy target for us. But reinforcements arrived. Although the weary Pakistani soldiers were impeded by the storms, we failed to achieve our objectives."

"And what became of you?"

"I was waiting for an opportunity to come home. I walked in the darkness of the night, scarcely a hundred paces, when I heard quick footsteps behind me. It was a dimly lit place. Then something heavy struck me on my head and knocked me out. When I opened my eyes, I didn't know who I was, where I was, or how long it had been since I was attacked. My head was wrapped up in a bandage, and I was lying in a hospital bed."

"I know the rest of the story from Shiraj. Do you know that he was the one who attended to your wounds?"

"Is it true? What a coincidence."

"What happened after that?"

"I escaped one day from the hospital, crossed into Indian borders, and began to live in anonymity. I made new friends in a small village that I settled down in, and I didn't mind what name they called me. I learned the trade of buying and selling. I carried on the best I could, not really sure who I was."

"Oh, Farzad. I cannot bear to think of you alone like that."

"I was a total stranger, but I did not remember my life before. I could not miss what I did not remember. But then I went to the fair with glass bangles. And there you were. All those memories came flooding back. I was overjoyed to see you alive and healthy. But you are married, someone else's wife."

"I brought your flute. You left it in the fields."

"I left it for you. Keep it."

"I want you to know how hard I looked for you, Farzad. I did not rush into marriage. After you disappeared . . . life was not easy for me either."

"I must leave now, Afsana. The students at their college reunion invited me to give a talk about my experiences during the war." He spoke brusquely, abrupt to the point of rudeness.

"Can we meet up again tomorrow before I leave?"

"I don't think we should, no," he answered.

"When then? Surely we can remain friends."

After a pause, he said, "Both you and I gave our days over to war efforts. Don't you think it's better for all of us now to ride upon the tides of good days that are coming in? Don't you wish you were free to start all over again?"

She stood for a moment, her heart racing frantically when at last she came to the realization that he was abandoning her. She thought she would be able to make a connection with him, but no, there was no connection. It seemed to her that years of separation had made him incapable of any kind of feeling.

"You're saying the most awful things, Farzad. Tell me what I ought to do?" Afsana asked him at last.

He turned to her quietly, took her cold hands into his own.

"What is done unfortunately cannot be undone. You must try to forget us. I am both grieved and happy for you from my heart. I wanted to say goodbye to you, and you've given us the chance that the war deprived us of. I want to begin a new life, and I don't want to look back. Try to forget me. Look how well it turned out for you. Shiraj loves you, and you have Razia. Don't throw that away on a sad old dream."

His eyes no longer shone upon her, his face no longer smiled at her eagerly, hungry for time with her. Her husband's once familiar looks of longing and desire had been replaced by the cold stare of someone she hardly knew. She could not have been his wife anymore, she realized. The war had beaten them both, transformed them into new people—strangers in each other's eyes. She remembered him on their wedding day, his gleaming golden outfit as he proudly rode across the city toward her.

Razia returned from playing at the park. "I'm hungry, Ammu. Can we eat soon?"

Afsana promptly stood up straight, as though she had been pulled up by the hair. She understood he was sending her away, there was no place for her near him. No, she ought to go away—and this at once. She deemed it prudent to leave Dhaka and retrace her steps while there was still time. She noticed a stirring within her, unfamiliar, something she'd never felt before—a yearning for the quiet, uncomplaining husband, who had given her everything and demanded nothing.

She wanted him as never before. But this resolution to return was much easier formed than executed. There was no denying she had done him an injustice. Would her kind, ever-understanding husband be able to find it in his heart to welcome her back after what she had done?

"Of course, my love. We will go eat." She turned and rested a hand on Farzad's arm. "I wish you all the best. Goodbye."

∼

Farzad startled when she touched his arm. Her voice had changed indeed, weaker, but still the voice that in old days—not so very old either—was the one voice that meant the whole world to him. For a single instant, his thoughts strayed away into the past, and the marvel of his first love came back to him. He looked down upon the soft hand that held his arm. He stared at the fingers, held with desperation. His heart awoke under that touch, like a sudden flash of light, bringing back happy moments. And sad. He recalled the last look that he had seen on her face at the door when they parted, her face conveying the anxiety of uncertainty about seeing him again. He remembered that he had turned away abruptly, that in his preoccupied state of mind, he had not spoken one soothing word to her.

Her voice now sounded like a mournful echo of his dead love. The days when he adored her, thought her the most beautiful woman he had ever seen, the days when he lived on in the bitterness of missing her gentle love for him, could not be revived again. And it occurred to him that he still had a moment to decide, only a brief moment now, whether to take her back or abandon her. In his heart, he could neither commit himself nor leave her. He was filled with the survivor's guilt that affected them both—he from his wartime experiences, she from her life experiences. He obstinately refused to listen to any words of explanation which might have softened his wounded and disappointed feelings. And he severed with one blow the tie that bound him to the only person he loved in this whole wide world, thus sacrificing his love to honor and dignity.

He took her hand off his arm and after a long pause, he spoke in a dangerously softened voice.

"Well, I will say goodbye, then." He turned and walked away.

Five

THE WAITING

alking home from his hospital shift, Shiraj felt fatigued by loneliness. Mild malaise took possession of him, and a forlorn sadness pervaded his senses. He stared at the vanishing sun. As the sunlit rooftops were glistening high over the shadows of the dying day, his contemplative mind had wandered off beyond the rooftops to where the waning sun a moment ago blazed in the western sky.

It was one of those summer evenings. The last glimpse of sunlight was followed by the closing-in darkness, when nothingness and fleeting shadows prevailed, a melancholy silence predominated. The evening brought feelings of isolation and hopelessness, which seemed, from without, to penetrate within.

He remained absorbed in its beauty and its mystery, bringing its message of repose not only for him but also to the birds who flocked home to their perches.

His desolation increased as he entered the vacant house. He still had not adjusted to the oddly quiet stillness that filled the space since his wife and daughter had left. It was profoundly painful to accept that there were no answers and nothing could soothe or fill that terribly anxious space within. A universal silence prevailed, the clamoring of the outside world hushed for a while, as though the house held its breath in anticipation of the return of normality. And the waiting was the hardest part.

Shiraj heaved a half-sigh and sat in his chair. Weary with the constant smothered feeling of dejection, he realized that he could only change his own behavior. His young blood was stirred with a longing, his young heart aflame. A feeling of warm, fiery love engulfed him as he waited in anticipation for someone close to his heart.

After a while, a sense of vague but sweet hopefulness brightened him up a little, softening his miseries. He did not know why, but hope raised its head and encouraged him to consider happy visions of a future. Although his cheeks appeared pale and there were dark shadows under his eyes, he seemed to have overcome all his fatigue.

What could Afsana be doing? Was she never coming back? Shiraj began to wonder, then realized he could not control whether or not she returned. He was not a man given to jealousy. Moreover, since the birth of Razia, there was a sense of security in his wife's fidelity. If only they would return, there was nothing left in this world he could ask for.

Sitting and stewing in his chair accomplished nothing. A sudden burst of energy overtook him, and he busied himself with some of the cozy rituals of the evening. He lit lamps in the darkened rooms, he pulled the shutters and drew the curtains. Just as he wandered to the kitchen to consider what to have for dinner, he thought he heard a gentle knock at the door. He stopped moving and listened, a little hesitant to believe his ears. He heard the knock again, and this time he hurried to the door, not wanting to miss whoever it was.

~

Afsana stood at the door of the cheerless home of hers, the drawn drapes and shutters closing in each lighted room, as if hiding what she had walked away from, taunting her by keeping her out. When no one responded to her gentle knock, she grew anxious. What if she was not allowed back in? She knocked loudly.

"Shiraj, let me in!" Afsana called. "Please, let me in."

The stillness of the night mocked her. Her mind spun out of control, envisioning a future in which Shiraj denied her return. She fisted both hands and pounded on the door.

Finally, she heard his voice. A voice that had grown so dear to her, so slowly and gently she had not even realized.

"Afsana!" he cried, unbolting the door and throwing it wide. "My own."

She longed for his tenderness, while fully expecting righteous anger and dejection.

"I want to come in. Please."

Shiraj stepped aside and waited as both mother and daughter filed in. He scooped his daughter into his arms and held her close. He appeared as calm and composed as usual, as if nothing had happened. She waited for the storm of anger to unleash.

He stood gazing upon her, his look mingled with curiosity and astonishment. He then took her hand and drew her closer, but she shrunk from him. Timidly, she raised her eyes to the man to whom she owed every blessing on this earth, the man to whom she owed all love and affection.

He looked upon her sternly, but it was the sternness of grief, not the sternness of resentment. Afsana leaned against the door for an instant, then launched herself at him. Tears flowing freely, she entreated him to forgive her, not to drive her away from him.

A dreaded silence followed. He allowed Razia to slide to the floor, resting her gently on her feet. She ran for her room.

Shiraj took Afsana in his arms, glanced around for the nearest chair, seated himself, and drew her onto his lap. He brushed the tangled hair from her brow.

"Why did you leave me, Afsana? You ran off without saying a word."

"I left a note for you, and I explained everything in it. But here I am, you see." She forced a shaky smile as tears rolled down her cheeks. She could not bear the loss of another husband, another life.

"Oh, Afsana, I had such hopes for us." He smiled weakly.

Had? That sounded bad. She heaved another sigh as fresh tears wetted his shirt.

"What is it, my love?" he asked gently.

Afsana looked up in surprise at the tender and anxious tone coming from him. At the touch of his kind and soothing words, she burst out sobbing as if her heart would break. And between her sobs, she told him everything, all the anguish of the past days. Her gasping sobs jumbled her words, making them nearly incomprehensible.

"I missed you so much, Afsana," Shiraj said in a low trembling tone.

"It was no reflection on you," she whispered. "No fault of your own. You have always been too good and too kind to me. It was my wayward nature. But I promise, I'll never leave you again."

He shook his head, but she could see how desperately he wanted to believe her.

"Never," she repeated fervently. "I'll never leave you again, Shiraj."

She saw with clarity how the years and all that they had gone through together had drawn them closer to one another, enabling them to grow beyond the past. She hoped their reconciliation was complete for him as well so they could re-establish their normal, peaceful relationship. Whatever short-lived longing for her past Farzad had stirred within her had been doused. The fiery passions of her youth had cooled, washed away by the glimpse of reality.

~

Shiraj couldn't resist the wan look on her dear face, the sadness of her smile. When he forgave her, he did so with his full heart, believing in his own words. The truth was, he hated himself for his weaknesses. So, he refrained from voicing his concerns and raising a painful discussion. He hid it all away in his heart.

Although Afsana flattered herself that she loved Shiraj, she had never loved him with that pure affection that she felt for Farzad. He saw it now. Why else would she have gone after him? Shiraj felt like a fool. Without seeming to, she played upon every feeling of his heart, drawing him nearer to her, completely under her influence.

He saw now that she had loved him as a vine clinging to the oak—its protector—whereas her love for Farzad was like a dewdrop on the flower to rejuvenate her. Shiraj loved Afsana with an intensity, a devotion, that she seemed to desire from her first husband, Farzad.

Shiraj's love for her had lost none of its fervor even though his spirit had been scathed. But he was unwilling to properly communicate his discontent, since it came at the risk of one of them finally walking away. And so he kept quiet to keep the peace.

But the cause of their estrangement, their first real strife, was not removed entirely. It festered like an open sore that had not healed completely, liable to break out again at the slightest irritation. A vague but deep-seated feeling of suspicion and distrust developed in Shiraj. Had she been toying with him all along? Simply playing upon his love for her and using him? The slight resentment grew, and with it an anger, and the thought of it sent the blood rushing hotly to his head, a strong desire to crush the fate that had so wantonly dangled happiness before him, only to take it away from him.

Instead of talking with his wife and searching for a resolution, he felt he needed to get off the emotional roller coaster. He thought it could be healthy for them to have time apart and remain separate individuals, helping them appreciate the time they were together even more. There was an opportunity in learning to live his life as best as he could outside of their relationship. He shared his plan with her over breakfast one morning, still not fully forthcoming with the reason behind his decision.

"I'm going to be busy for some time," he said. "I'll be gone for a few days and continue my voluntary service at the refugee camp. They are always short of hands at the camp."

Shiraj left the house and worked long hours to divert his mind.

Afsana watched Shiraj leave, then ran to her room, exhausted by the worry that, while her husband voiced forgiveness, something in him continued to build a wall between them. No matter how she attempted to make up for her foolish flight to Dhaka, he could not fully forgive her. Ironically, she loved him more deeply now than she ever had before.

She fought against the impulse to remind him of the time jealousy had stirred within her, when her friend Nafisa had developed feelings for him. And yet, she knew it was not the same. He had done nothing to prompt it. Even then, Shiraj had acted only with kindness and generosity and encouraged nothing untoward.

She lay weeping on the bed. Nobody would ever know what she went through, she thought, her agonies would be buried with her in her grave. How would Shiraj feel about her if he knew her darkest secrets? Would his protective nature be stirred? Or would disgust overtake all else? She had never wanted to find out and certainly didn't feel more inclined now.

Her return to Dhaka had reminded her how sorely she missed her parents, how her life had been shattered in a matter of days. She was reminded of what would have become of her had Shiraj not intervened. If she had to face other mishaps in life, she had no one in the world to turn to, save Shiraj whom she had affronted and forsaken. Like a wounded animal, she'd crept back to the only home she knew, her own home, the home she and Shiraj had created together. She wanted the solidity and permanence of her house, her life. But she could not entirely rid her mind of the look on his face, unnatural, ghastly, like a persecuted man. And now that she was alone, she felt as if she were haunted.

A week later, a long week with each passing day creating more concern that her life was taking another drastic turn, Shiraj returned. She and Razia heard the knock on the door. Afsana feared to hope, but Razia ran for the door and threw it open.

He appeared calm, fully composed. As he walked through the door, Razia gave him a hug. He picked her up and said, "How's my angel Razia?"

Looking at them both, there was a surge of new love in Afsana's heart. This man's devotion to their daughter melted her heart anew.

She also came to the realization that, despite how he might feel about Afsana, Shiraj would not want to give up Razia. She must have been a fool to forsake the love of a man who was ready to do anything for her child. Razia, her little daughter, must be protected and loved at any cost.

Again she realized how fortunate she had been in finding Shiraj at the refugee camp. It was he who offered his good heart, his honest hands. He might stay now for Razia, but she would win back his affection. She would throw herself into this marriage with utmost care, doting on him until he remembered his love for her and forgot her one indiscretion. She would never again take him for granted or consider him second. Not to anyone.

Brimming with this determination, she took his hands in hers and looked into his eyes. "Shiraj, you are my one and only love. Thank you so much for everything you have done for me and for Razia. I don't know what I would do without you. Will you ever forgive me?"

She hoped that it was not too late for them. To her great relief, she saw Shiraj gazing at her with warmth and tender feelings in his eyes. He extended an arm to her. She rushed to him. Razia joined them in a family embrace. Afsana knew she had come home.

Six

DHAKA DAYS

1970

Afsana sat in class, listening to the professor drone on and on. She longed to join Farzad under the shade of the banyan tree to enjoy the warming weather of spring. Finally, the professor ended his lecture and dismissed the students. She gathered her notebook and hurried to meet Farzad.

He waited for her under the big banyan tree—the tree she thought of as "their" tree, for that was where he first approached her outside of class.

"Are you studying?" he had asked. "May I join you?"

Though first they focused on their notes and preparing for the difficult exams of their shared classes, soon their conversations became more personal, then intimate. Influenced by the excitement of revolutionary fervor that swept the country, Farzad preferred politics to law. Afsana spent whole Sunday afternoons in discussion of public law and history, thrilling to his passion. She could not help but be swayed by his arguments and drawn to join him in supporting the cause.

This afternoon, sitting beneath their tree, Afsana watched as

Farzad railed against their political leaders. She noticed for the first time how lovely his eyes were when he was fired up about something.

Farzad clenched a fist. "Our classes are so dull and fill me with such boredom. How can we care about the letter of the law when our people are subjugated? We study law but lack freedom. I want to make real change in this world. Politics is the way to change."

Afsana agreed with him. She would have agreed with anything he said, she realized, her heart fluttering just from his nearness. When did they become more than classmates? More than friends? Did he feel the same? He turned to look at her, mouth open to continue his argument, when she saw something change in the way he looked at her. He closed his mouth and swallowed hard. He took a breath. She held hers, skin prickling with the anticipation of what he was about to say.

"Afsana! Hello!" Nafisa waved from across the campus lawn and quickened her steps to join them. Her brother Nasir was beside her. The siblings were good friends of theirs. Normally, Afsana would delight in their company. But today she was sure they had interrupted something important. When she looked back at Farzad, the spark she had seen in his eyes moments ago was gone.

Nafisa flopped onto the ground beside Afsana. "How was class?"

"Professor Roy knows so much. But I wish he was a little more exciting."

"What are you writing?"

"An essay for a competition. Farzad encouraged me to enter. He says my writing is good." She blushed as she shared Farzad's praise.

"No, I said your writing is *excellent*," Farzad amended. "And I believe we can use this to our benefit."

Nasir stood beside Farzad. "We need something for the next batch of posters. Something to catch attention."

Farzad pointed to her. "She's your girl. Will those be ready next week? I want to hang one in Madhur's Canteen the next time we go."

"Then they will be ready," Nasir said. "Bengalis have a right to govern ourselves. West Pakistan is about to learn the same lesson France learned during the French Revolution."

"A fair comparison," Farzad agreed. "If they will not learn to listen to us, to treat us as equals with the same rights, then we have no choice but to separate. Bengali citizens have a right to representation in their government."

"And why should West Pakistan enjoy the benefits of our labor and taxes while denying us a voice in how those resources are distributed?"

"Exactly."

"But will it come to war?" Nafisa asked. "I don't think anyone ever wins in war."

"If it comes to that, so be it," Farzad said. "Independence will be worth the fight."

Afsana was not as sure as Farzad, but she did not argue. His passion had convinced her the struggle would be worth it. The students at Dhaka University needed to know they would have jobs after graduation, that they would have a say in their government.

"The fall of Dhaka Cantonment last year should have signaled them to take us more seriously," Nasir said. "We may be students, but we will not stop until our voices are heard."

Farzad nodded furiously. "Exactly so. We have proven we have the strength and resilience to stand against tyranny."

"I'll finish the posters. We can all four hang them around the city, the university. And of course the Canteen," Nasir said.

"See you there next week."

～

Madhur's Canteen was a place where the streets widened to make room for creative minds. The walls were covered with political graffiti and posters, the hangout was always noisy and packed. But Farzad managed to find enough space to hang their newest poster, proclaiming *Joy Bangla* above an image of Sheikh Mujibur Rahman, the leader of the Awami League party.

Like a fresco, the canteen's ceiling was painted in green and red, the colors of their national flag, stretching from east to west. Hundreds of people had crammed into the space tonight. Afsana held onto Farzad's arm as they squeezed through the smoky space, jostled by other like-minded revolutionaries who reached out to shake Farzad's hand or to clasp his shoulder in solidarity.

Afsana spotted Nafisa and Nasir and waved them over. All four of them pushed forward through the crowd to a back corner where their fellow students gathered. Nasir whispered into his sister's ear and nudged her toward another table a little farther away, where a young, charming, enthusiastic man busily scribbled on a piece of paper. He had started attending the meetings recently, but Afsana did not know him. She and Farzad followed their two friends.

"Farzad," Nasir said, "allow me to introduce you to Saif. He is from the town Nafisa and I grew up in and is favored by our parents. So favored in fact, that they have just consented to the engagement of Saif to my own sister, Nafisa. He shall soon be my brother."

Afsana squeezed Nafisa's hand. "You did not tell me!"

Nafisa looked ready to cry. "I did not know!"

Farzad grabbed Saif's hand and shook it vigorously. "We welcome you as a brother."

Nafisa sat quietly with Afsana. "I did not dare hope they would choose Saif for me," she confided. "And I had no idea they had chosen."

Nasir joined them at the table. "Are you happy, my sister?" he asked, eyes twinkling.

"So happy."

"I grew weary of Ammu's constant worry about 'Who will marry Nafisa' and 'When will this be decided' so I sat down with them and urged them to make a decision. When they asked me what I thought of Saif, I told them he would be my first choice for you."

Nafisa threw her arms around Nasir. "Thank you! I am so happy!"

"That is all I wanted."

Saif smiled at them, sending a pink blush blooming across Nafisa's cheeks. Nasir took Farzad and Saif to make the rounds of their fellow students, leaving the young women alone.

Afsana loved seeing her best friend glowing. "There is no denying your true happiness. You knew Saif?"

"Since we were young," Nafisa said. "I knew my parents were growing anxious about my marriage. And the anxiety was spilling over to Nasir. This must be why he traveled home last weekend. And why he was so mysterious about it."

"My parents have been accepting marriage proposals as well. I am trying not to discuss it yet. We have not even completed our studies."

"But how will you live without a husband?" Nafisa asked. "I confess I am relieved to know my match has been made. I am also thrilled that I know the man who will be my husband and even like him. But having the issue settled is the biggest relief of all. You must be causing your parents such heartache."

"I am certain I will find a husband," Afsana murmured.

Nafisa watched Afsana's gaze drift to Farzad and smiled. "Or perhaps your heart has already found the one it wants."

Afsana sighed. "But my parents do not know Farzad as yours know Saif. If the *ghatak* does not bring him as a possible match, how can I ask them to consider him?"

"They will love him. He is smart and is helping lead a revolution. And how wonderful if we were both engaged! Perhaps even get married soon."

Afsana watched as Farzad charmed and mesmerized the other students. They hung on every word he said. Could Nafisa be correct? Would her parents see Farzad as favorably as she and Nafisa did?

She listened eagerly over endless piping hot cups of tea while Farzad talked about his hopes and dreams of an independent country, free from the shackles of the despotic rulers of West Pakistan. For hours, they sat next to each other, Farzad's low, sweet voice uttering words of wondrous fascination, inspiring others with his vision of a Bengali nation. With the talk of engagements and marriage, Afsana's thoughts swirled to her future, lifting her to a heady excitement.

The evening ended with promises of meeting again next week, everyone sure of the future Farzad described so beautifully.

Farzad walked her back to her room on campus whenever their activities kept them out late at night. That night, he took her hand in his. She continued forward without saying a word, eyes ahead, afraid any misunderstood look or word might discourage him and result in him letting go. She reveled in his touch. His eyes, like stars, beamed with splendor when he looked at her. She could not have broken the spell that enthralled her.

At her door, he paused, taking both hands in his. "Afsana, you must know how I feel about you. We are more than like-minded students now, are we not? I know we spend most of our time working toward common goals, but I would like to be more than that."

"I feel the same, Farzad." She squeezed his hands.

He smiled and bid her goodnight. After she eased the door closed, she leaned against it, her heart racing, barely able to breathe.

Seven

TYING THE KNOT

Afsana received a letter from her mother that week, letting her know her father had received an excellent name from the *ghatak,* the matchmaker, as a suitable candidate for her future husband.

Her heart beat wildly. She had never mentioned Farzad to her parents. How would they respond? *Ghataks* were expensive but necessary for arranged marriages. That was tradition. She tucked the letter away, knowing she needed to speak up. On the other hand, Farzad had said nothing of marriage. She could not tell her parents about something that did not exist.

She met Farzad under the banyan tree after class, eager to show him her latest slogan and illustrations for the posters. They took a long stroll around the riverbank. Farzad tossed a small pebble into the water, sending little waves of emotion beyond the immediate set of circumstances. It brought about a change in the mood.

"Did you bring your flute?" Afsana asked.

"Yes, I remembered to bring it this time."

Afsana sat by Farzad's feet and basked in the evening glow of the setting sun while listening to his music. Though she raised her voice regularly in crowds, making her political views known, she hadn't yet been able to open her mouth around her parents to tell them about her budding relationship with Farzad.

They had been together for a while now, but though she knew he showed no interest in other women, she was not sure if he felt as deeply connected to her as she did to him. She still was not sure where this was going, if it would be long term, if he was "the one." Discussing the subject of marriage with Farzad was more difficult than confiding to her parents that she had entered into a relationship with a man they knew nothing about.

In order to gauge his interest, Afsana started a general conversation, dropping hints to test the waters and see if they were on the same page.

"My parents have enlisted a *ghatak* to find matches for me," she said, unable to look at him. He stopped playing his flute. "Whenever they start talking about marriage, I am so embarrassed and don't know what to say. I told them I am still too young to get married."

"I, too, am tired of my mother and her matchmaking friends. They want me to marry a suitable girl of their choice. I told them that if I marry, it will be a woman of my own choosing. But they are relentless."

"At least you told them that much. I shudder to think how my parents would react if I said something so bold. Whenever my mother speaks to me, she has only one topic." Afsana intoned a higher pitch, feigning her mother's bossy tone. "Afsana, don't you realize it is time to settle down, get married, and start a family? When will you stop wasting time at school? At a certain age a girl must be married.'"

Farzad's lips twisted into a lopsided smile. "That has been tradition. And how do they feel about you attending political rallies, crying out for independence?"

"God, I do not mention our activities. I only tell them how boring class is. My father will say, 'I don't see any point in continuing school. I am spending so much money on the matchmaker.

She is bringing excellent proposals for you but you are not showing any interest!'"

His head whipped around to face her, his eyebrows knitted together. "She has already brought proposals to your parents?"

Afsana laughed as if she found the entire thing a joke. But her heart thumped. "My mother has dreamy hopes of me marrying a perfect groom and living happily ever after."

Farzad rose onto his knees. "And what is your dreamy hope, Afsana? If you marry and leave university, what becomes of us . . . of our hopes and dreams?"

She drank in his features, afraid of losing him, of never seeing him again. His stormy dark eyes, always on fire with his passions. His cheekbones and jaw, always set as if ready for a deep discussion. His red lips, soft and normally smiling, now turned down in reflection of his concern. How often had she dreamed of kissing those lips?

"I do not want that, Farzad, but what can I tell them?"

He took her hands. "Can you tell them you have met someone?"

Her palms dampened with sweat as she whispered, "But no one has asked me to marry them."

"Afsana, you can tell them truly that you have found a man who would take you as his wife for the rest of his life." He walked to the water's edge and plucked the flower from a blooming water lily, which he presented to her on one knee. "Afsana, I want you by my side forever. Will you marry me?"

Tears sprang to her eyes as her dream unfolded before her. "Yes, Farzad! My love!" She threw her arms around him, careful not to crush the lily.

"But, Afsana, we have to meet and converse with our parents to seek their approval and blessings," Farzad said. "I will not ask my wife to defy her family."

He wrapped his hand over hers. She looked down and wrapped her fingers around his.

The anxiety gripping her heart eased. With Farzad by her side, she could do anything.

"I agree with you, Farzad. We can travel home together. I will introduce you to my parents, and you introduce me to your parents. We can have a frank conversation with them and allow them to voice their objections if they have any. If we remain calm and behave maturely, this may alleviate fears that we're marrying too quickly, marrying for the wrong reasons, or marrying the wrong person."

What a relief to be able to share her secret with her parents. No longer would she need to squirm in discomfort as she turned down one proposal after another. Now if only they could convince their parents they were good together. If she could face her parents on this issue, she could face anything life threw at her.

Afsana thought perhaps she was the luckiest woman in the world. Some secret part of her never believed her parents would agree to a marriage they did not arrange. Nor did she expect them to give their blessings to a man Afsana had selected on her own behalf. But because Afsana and Farzad were from the same city—though had not known each other well—and the families were familiar with each other, her father nodded his head. He did not even grumble too much about having paid money to the *ghatak*.

Her mother pinched her cheeks. "Now you will be a proper bride."

And then, wonder of wonders, Farzad's family extended their approval to the union as well. Afsana's mother nearly shook with excitement. "We have a wedding to plan!"

With political turmoil swirling around them, Afsana reveled in the excitement and diversion of the wedding. A whirlwind of activities took over her days.

The engagement was formalized through *paka-dekha*. Both families gathered at the groom's parents' house to decide the date and time of the wedding. Farzad's parents served an assortment of sweets, as well as *paan-chini*, betel leaf with areca nuts, presented with silver foil to signify the festive nature of the gathering. After *paka-dekha*, the engagement was formally announced to their friends and relatives.

A week before the wedding, the elders of Farzad's family came to bless Afsana by sprinkling husked rice and trefoil on her head. They gave her gifts of gold jewelry, clothes, and sweets. Afsana's family followed suit and blessed the groom in the same manner.

Afsana's relatives, including some distant ones whom she had not seen for years, traveled to attend her wedding. This was an occasion where generations of people who hardly got a chance to get together came to a single venue. As they gathered, they remembered the good old days and recounted their memories of growing up and of previous celebrations. They marveled at how grown up Afsana was now, when they remembered her as a little girl.

Her parents' home nearly burst at the seams trying to house so many guests. They were so excited that no one minded the cramped space or spending the night in makeshift beds. Bedsheets were rolled up into pillows. Some just slept on a *khatiya charpai* bed, a cot of sorts, with sacked jute rope crisscrossed to lie on. Bamboo sleeping mats were unrolled each night on open patches of floor. The hustle and bustle and the sleeping arrangements were all part of the fun of having the whole family together. Jokes and laughter continued all night long. Afsana loved every moment.

Anxiety and stress built when Afsana realized she had only a few days before the event that her family had been planning for months. After all of the planning was done, she became teary eyed over seeing/hearing/talking about anything wedding related. She felt as if she was forgetting something, so she laid in bed at night unable to sleep. She began to have pre-wedding jitters, a feeling of nervousness, worry, and apprehension as this important transition of her life came closer. She didn't doubt her feelings for Farzad, but the realization she would leave her parents' house weighed heavily. This huge change would upheave everything in her life.

But then began the three days leading up to the ceremony. Afsana barely had time to breathe, much less worry.

Afsana's henna night was her special night, when her friends and family members she grew up with gathered to eat, dance, and sing—a lively tradition for the women only. They all dressed in their most beautiful dresses, danced, and of course painted each other's hands with the reddish-brown henna. It was a part of sixteen steps recommended by ancient texts to prepare a bride for her new life. Not only was it considered to bring luck, joy, and beauty, but also the scent was said to have aphrodisiac properties. And it soothed the body and prevented the nerves from becoming tense.

Her mother broke the *mehendi* brought by the groom's family into a copper bowl. After the breaking of the *mehendi*, she mixed it into a paste, mashing it together with various oils, lemon, and tea to enhance the intensity and longevity of the color. An old saying claimed that the darker the color of the bride's henna, the deeper the husband's love for her. Afsana could tell her mother was determined that no one at her wedding would doubt Farzad's love for his bride.

Her mother draped her in a veil and escorted her to the middle of a circle. Nafisa, who was already betrothed, was the first to apply the prepared henna on Afsana's palm. One of Afsana's younger cousins applied the same on the other palm. The henna was then offered to all the ladies who had gathered. During the henna ritual, traditional folk music was played, but afterward it turned into a never-ending party of dancing until the morning.

The morning of her wedding, Afsana woke to a beautiful day,

nervous but pleased that her anxiety was gone. She smiled, knowing tonight she would be Farzad's wife. The entire day was devoted to preparing her to be the most beautiful bride she could be. She would not leave the house the entire day, not until after the ceremony, when she would leave with Farzad to begin their life together.

Gaye holud was an intimate ceremony. All the female members of her family gathered to spread turmeric paste over her body to give her skin a bridal glow. Five, seven, or nine (it needed to be odd numbers) married women made the turmeric paste out of raw turmeric sticks using grinding stones. Her mother rubbed her forehead and cheeks with turmeric paste, then all the relatives took turns massaging the paste on her face and body.

Everyone wore yellow outfits as the paste would stain any fabric it came into contact with. Afsana wore a simple yellow cotton saree as she was going to be bathed to remove the turmeric from all over her face and body. An entire tray containing a huge, decorated Rohu fish symbolizing fertility, good fortune, and wisdom was sent by Farzad's family along with turmeric. The fish had been cooked in a time-honored tradition and would be distributed amongst close relatives who were present on that day.

Although she felt a little bashful about the traditional purification and cleansing ceremony, she enjoyed the comfort and support of her extended family. It was an unforgettable experience to be pampered and loved, and it made her feel special.

Unaccustomed to being the center of so much attention, Afsana found herself a bundle of nerves and escaped to her room. The person she needed most—her mother—joined her and continued to fuss over her daughter. She leaned forward, as if sharing something conspiratorial.

"I am so excited about your wedding tonight and want to touch base with you on getting ready. Would you like me to be close by as you get dressed and ready? If not, I understand."

"Ammu," Afsana replied, "I want you to be here with me. I'm already stressed out and need you to stay by my side. Nafisa will be here soon. I can ask her to do your hair and makeup in addition to mine. She is quite good."

"Sounds good to me. Is Nasir coming too?"

"Oh yes. He wouldn't miss my wedding. I know that for sure."

"Good. Let's go greet the guests as they arrive. That will be better than sitting here fretting."

Guests continued to stream into the home. Finally, the door opened to reveal Nafisa in a glittering saree. With Nasir at her side, they navigated through the crowd, everybody's attention on them.

"Isn't this a very enchanting evening?" Nasir said. "Everybody's looking beautiful and handsome, looking very happy. Truly, this is a celebration of life and love."

Nafisa hugged her. "Are you ready for me to style your hair? Oh, I am so excited for you! And to think, in about a month, we will be celebrating my wedding to Saif."

"I am so glad you are here. I have been such a bundle of nerves," Afsana confided.

"Whatever about? You love Farzad."

"I do. And I wanted this so badly. I—"

The sound of drums and horns alerted them to Farzad's approach. The *borjatri*, or the procession that marked the groom's arrival at the bride's home, was a most joyous occasion. All of Afsana's family poured outside to watch. Farzad looked dashing in his gold *sherwani* with a scarf that matched Afsana's. He rode a bedecked car, sent by Afsana's parents, driven by a chauffeur. It rolled at a slow speed, so that he could be escorted by his friends and relatives in a procession, the musicians playing their instruments, singing songs and dancing. Farzad's family carried huge trays of sweets, the bride's wedding outfit, jewelry, cosmetics, and gifts for the bride's family.

Farzad's mother stepped forward and handed Afsana the

wedding saree and jewelry that she would wear this evening. Her eyes sparkled with happiness. "Welcome, daughter. I wish you and my son all future happiness."

Finally, she was ready to don her bridal outfit. Nafisa and her mother joined her to assist. She raised her arms above her head and her mother helped her in draping the red silk saree in the Bengali style by draping the *pallu* over the left shoulder and pleating the rest of the saree in a unique way. This style was perfect if you wanted to add a traditional touch to your look. Just donning a saree would be incomplete without the right kind of jewelry to match the outfit. So she added a pair of *jhumkas* (intricate dangling earrings), a necklace, and a set of bangles. A diamond nose stud was her finishing touch.

Besides gold jewelry, Afsana adorned herself in a long garland to be exchanged later with Farzad's garland during the wedding ceremony.

Afsana knew that while she dressed, her father welcomed Farzad with sherbet and sprinkled rose water on his family. She could hear the excitement bubbling in the exuberant conversations that carried through the house. The moment she heard Farzad's voice and knew he was in the house, ready to take her as his bride, her stomach unclenched. She looked at herself in the mirror, hoping he would be pleased.

The *nikah*, or the wedding, then commenced. The bride and the groom were seated in two different areas along with family and friends of the same gender and a *maulavi* who asked both if they accepted the other as their partner. After confirming their acceptance, they signed the wedding documents. Their love was official. Later Farzad and his father along with the Afsana's father would meet to sign the official *mehr* contract, giving the bride a set amount of money as her dowry.

The newlyweds were seated together for the first time as man and wife, to take part in numerous traditions, including drinking from the same glass in order to 'increase their love for one another' as the old belief went. They exchanged garlands made of fresh flowers, to bring them close to each other. There was music and dance, food was served to the guests.

The next evening, the newly married left for the groom's house. Afsana waved goodbye to her mother and father, a mixture of excitement and sadness swirling through her.

When they arrived, Farzad introduced his wife to all his distant relatives. As Afsana stood at the center of this festive occasion, smiling and greeting each new family member, she couldn't help but notice how Farzad radiated joy and pride. His excitement was contagious. She felt her own build as they embarked upon a new journey and all the good things that life had in store for them. Basking in his glow, she feared nothing.

If only she knew how quickly it would all fall apart.

Eight

THE LOST YEARS

1971

Afsana and Farzad made their home in Dhaka after the wedding. But before she knew what was happening, Farzad announced he needed to leave. They had been married only a few weeks. She knew that Farzad was an active member of a nascent student separatist group. He had never hidden this, though he didn't share his late-night activities. She had hoped he would come to see her as more important than his cause, that they would have time together. But the early magic of their relationship was never given the chance to blossom into marital bliss.

She was aware that young men like him were always in danger of being picked up by the West Pakistani army and the loyalist forces. Sometimes his comrades would go missing for days. Some would be gone for a week and return bruised, physically and mentally deranged. And some were never seen again.

Once he left, Afsana struggled to adapt to life alone. This was not the life she had envisioned for them. Every day, she went about her tasks, trying to focus but constantly hoping for surprise visits. She listened every moment for the squeak of the back door, the unlatching of the hinge, or unexpected footsteps in the corridor.

Nights were the worst. The little window beside her bed offered an extended view over the streets beneath. Heart still fluttering with fear, yet a strange joy predominating her senses, she would sit by the window, watching for a shadow to emerge and morph into the shape of her husband.

The smallest sound of footsteps or voices of people in the streets below made her tremble with excitement. If rain set in, she waited patiently for it to subside, returning to her watch once the sky cleared. Week after week, she kept up her belief he would return to her. Each night, her heart broke anew when he did not. And yet, each day, as the light began to wane, she looked out yet again, fully expecting that this would be the night her Farzad would return.

While waiting and watching for Farzad one night, she became aware of some strange stirring outside. When she looked up, she saw in the darkening sky a jet of bright flames, like fiery tongues bursting out of a smoldering building, piercing the roof. She heard a huge explosion, together with a distant roar of voices.

A storage depot of ammunition was in flames.

The *Mukti Joddhas*, the freedom fighters, were nearby.

Her ears perked at the slight creak of a door opening. She gathered her nightgown close to her body, her breath coming in quick gasps. Was someone in the house? She would be trapped in this bedroom if West Pakistani soldiers broke in and found her alone. Glancing around, she confirmed what she already knew—that there was no place to hide.

She looked up fearfully as her bedroom door squeaked—a hand controlled by a dark figure pushed it open.

As he stepped into the light, Afsana realized this was the night and the moment she had been longing for.

"You frightened me, Farzad," she said.

In the darkness of the room, Farzad reached her side. He traced the contours of her face with his fingertips, keeping his touch gentle.

"Soldiers are in town," she warned him. "It isn't safe for you here." The joy of finally seeing her husband was overshadowed by the fear of him being apprehended.

He leaned forward and kissed her. "Afsana, my beloved, it is my one and only dream to be with you tonight. What is death compared to a night with my beautiful wife."

A quiet sigh escaped from her as she sprang forward and clasped him in her arms, her aching heart beating anew. She laid her head on his shoulder. Her hands slowly went up to his hair as she sobbed out her joy and sorrow.

He led her to the bed. Her robe and nightgown slid off more easily than his clothing. She waited for him to join her, then nestled against his warm skin.

He held her in the quiet hush of the night. A moment of complete satisfaction carried her to bliss. But it was far from perfect. The anticipation of separation already engulfed her heart.

"You cannot stay, can you?"

She felt his body tense.

"I'm going to have to leave, Afsana," he whispered, his arms tightening their embrace. "And this time, I won't be nearby. I'll come back for you when it is safe."

She clutched him to her. "No, you will not go tonight. You will wait and rest with me till morning."

"Nothing but absolute necessity could compel me to leave you now. But my love, I have no choice but to leave you. We have worked too hard for our freedom to quit now. This is for you and me. For our children and their children."

"Our children?" Afsana blushed, envisioning a young version of Farzad, a little boy with his brilliant eyes and sure smile.

"And all children in the future."

"Don't go. Please don't. Or if you go, let me come with you."

"You can't, my love. It's too dangerous. You will be safer here."

When his words faltered, he pressed his lips to her hand.

"We must not meet more than is strictly necessary," he warned her.

"Of course. I will do nothing to endanger you," she replied.

"You are the reason I fight for freedom and my reason to come back. And I will return to you no matter what. Don't worry."

She clutched him tightly and cried.

"Don't make the pain of parting worse than it already is." His voice trembled a little as he buried his face in her hair.

"Promise me you will come back soon." She held him as though she would never let go.

"I promise. You talk as if I am going away forever. After the war, we'll be together again. Together in the free Bengali nation we fought to establish. We will have incredible stories for our children."

"Farzad," she moaned.

He gently unhooked her arms and pulled away. He dressed quickly. "I advise you not to stay in town another day. Return to your parents and stay with them until I can once again be by your side."

She dried her cheeks. "I will be strong for you. I promise."

"I had better go." He bent to kiss her one last time. She grabbed him and refused to let go. He straightened and tore himself from her embrace. "Goodbye."

She jumped up and pulled her robe about her to see him to the door. He did not look back, but left in a rush, swinging open the door and hurrying out into the darkness of the night.

She followed him with her eyes until he disappeared.

"Do not forget me when we are apart. Trust me with all your heart," she said to no one.

Nine

OPERATION SEARCHLIGHT

Afsana returned to her parents' home after Farzad left her. About a week had passed—a long, lonely week of missing her new husband. She had not once heard from Farzad and had no idea where he had gone. A piece of herself had gone with him, and she spent every moment of her days trying to fill the empty place.

She frequently sat on the grass in the back of her parents' house, under the enormous mango tree that covered and shaded the whole of it. When the wind sprang up, the great mass of fallen leaves would rise, rustling into the air. Ripened mangoes thudded senselessly to the ground. She loved the house where she had grown up, attached as she was by deep roots. Her ancestors had been born and died here, and she was anchored by their lingering presence, by the very atmosphere itself.

On March 25th, 1971, evening crept in surreptitiously, like a betrayer. Afsana inhaled deeply and could almost smell a different night. Around dusk, she watched in awe at the crazy swooping and swirling of hundreds and hundreds of birds flying in the sky. As if in warning, they issued a low murmur from thousands of wingbeats and their soft cries. A warm wind split apart a sinister sky far on the horizon—waiting to unfold the fate of the darkest night in the history of Bangladesh.

She heard a strange hum, a very deep and quiet rumble, a bit like a distant drill. It churned in the distance, at first quiet but steady, then suddenly a full roar. As it neared, it changed into a squealing sound of metal on metal. She felt a vibration that almost instantly increased in intensity.

The window in her bedroom shook and rattled. She heard glasses in the kitchen begin to clink, shuddering with the rumbling. Her wedding photo, which hung on the wall of her bedroom, rattled on its hook and fell to the floor, shattering and littering the floor with glass shards. On the tiny table in her room where she took tea, the cup trembled on the saucer and the leg of the table jostled against her knee.

Loud clanking made her run to look out of the window. A column of tanks chugged along the streets of Dhaka, belching black smoke. Beyond the dusty roads, people of the neighborhood had gathered in small groups, talking in great agitation. She could not distinguish any details of their faces in the dark. She heard a sound like firecrackers going off then, all of a sudden, a metallic rattling—what sounded like a machine gun. People started screaming and dropping to the ground. Some tried to save the injured ones, but the ceaseless gunshots sent them running for safety.

The West Pakistani troops had arrived. Afsana stepped away from the window.

She ran to find her parents. The three of them huddled together, silently listening to the assault outside. Her father listed off a number of places they could seek refuge, concerned about being trapped in a war zone. But they could not leave in the middle of this pandemonium. They remained awake all night, hoping for a break in the onslaught.

In the morning, things quieted briefly.

When fists pounded on the door, Afsana clutched her

mother and father, terrified of the soldiers who must be the cause.

"Go to your room and hide," her father instructed, rising to answer the call. "And both of you throw some things into a bag. Be ready to run."

Afsana did as she was told. Until she heard female voices and ran back to her father's side.

Her father opened the door just a crack, enough to peek outside, then threw it wide.

Two of her college friends tumbled into the house. Her mother rushed forward to the terrified young women.

"We did not know where else to go," one of them gasped after Afsana's father closed and locked the door.

"It is okay. You are safe here," Afsana's mother assured them.

Afsana was shocked to see her friends in their current state, smeared with grime, eyes wild with confusion.

"Dhaka University is under attack. They set fire to the ladies' hostel, trying to force us all out."

Her other friend burst into a fit of coughing. "You are lucky you married and moved out. We had nowhere to take cover."

"The faculty and students have been most vocal about calling for a free Bangladesh," Afsana's father said. "The Pakistanis must hope to silence the movement."

Afsana clutched her chest, wondering where Farzad was now. Was he fighting in this onslaught, even as she listened to fellow students recount the horrors they'd seen?

"You can stay with us," Afsana told them. "And flee with us. We were just packing to leave."

Their eyes widened and they shook their heads. "No! You can't leave now. Stay safe in your home. The entire city is under attack. I woke up to a deafening sound followed by a succession of blasts. I've never heard anything like it. I was so terrified that I did not know what I should do. Some of the students ran for the roof to take shelter there. I don't know what happened to them. I crawled into one of the restrooms to hide."

Her other friend coughed again. "I was there too, and we huddled under the sinks, listening to the shellfire and the screaming. But then we smelled smoke. We had to sneak out of the hostel. Soldiers were moving through the building, room by room, shining flashlights into every dark space and grabbing anyone flushed out by the fire. They found a few students and professors hiding. We watched them drag them outside and shoot them. The sound of gunfire and pleas for mercy are still in my ears. I will never forget it."

"After we made it out of the hostel, we crept across campus. We saw Professor Roy dragged from his living quarters and stabbed with a bayonet when he tried to resist."

"Professor Roy?" The brilliant man would never again bore a class of students. Afsana closed her eyes against the image, trying to hold back tears.

"People cut down trees along the streets and formed barricades to try to hold off the army. They gathered push carts, old cars, empty oil barrels, tar barrels, anything to create an obstacle on the path of the army, that just keep advancing into the neighborhoods."

"Those trees were hundreds of years old!" Afsana wondered if her banyan tree would survive the assault, or if it was already cut down.

"As we snuck across town, we saw dead bodies piled up on the sides of the roads—" Afsana's friend collapsed, unable to speak any more.

Afsana tried to call her uncle, a newspaper reporter, but the phone was dead. She suspected the advancing army had cut the lines to leave the people powerless to call for help. Outside, the city had become like a ghost town, the streets deserted, an eerie calm settling after the night's brutal assault. The five of them stayed inside the rest of the day and into the night. Lying in her bed in the dark, Afsana heard the whistle of bullets and the yelping of men.

On the morning of March 27th, her father ventured out to

see what was happening and to attempt to get some food for them all. He came back completely distraught and shared that his office had been set on fire. There was blood on his shirt, and the area around one of his eyes was swollen and turning black. When Afsana's mother pulled his shirt off his back, it was covered with welts.

"What happened to you? Who did this?" she asked.

"The loyalists are everywhere. They are trying to save themselves by giving up freedom fighters. They hit me and tried to pick me up."

Afsana's mother gasped. "Our neighbors did this to you?"

"Last night they also attacked Madhu's Canteen. Poor Madhu, he and his family were all brutally murdered in the raid. Some of the men attempted to resist the attack, but the few who fought back were nothing compared to the invaders. We can't stay here. Not any longer. They'll come for all of us. We must leave at once."

They shut all the doors and windows and huddled together in the living room for hours. Afsana later learned that her uncle, the newspaper reporter, left his house in fear and went into hiding. His house was raided, and when the soldiers found no one there, they shot the pets instead.

The next morning, before they had a chance to flee, Afsana heard hurried footsteps, then insistent knocks, followed by pounding. She shot straight up in bed, her heart racing. That sound—it was like someone had kicked the door in and entered the house by force.

She joined her parents in the main room of the home and could see numerous military vehicles in front of their house.

"What do you want?" Afsana confronted the men.

"Where is your husband?" they demanded.

"He is not here and has not been. I have no idea where he is."

"We tracked you down here and have orders to search this house."

Afsana watched helplessly as the soldiers pilfered all the personal belongings in the home. They did not simply search, nor did they appear to be actively looking for Farzad. They rifled through her clothing and fell upon her wedding jewelry with delight. Her stomach churned, seeing the beloved pieces that had graced her body such a short time ago rough-handled and shoved into pockets. Ironically, she had brought it with her for safekeeping. Every chest of drawers was opened and dumped out, every closet emptied of treasured belongings. Photos were yanked from the walls. Cushions torn up. They ransacked everything in the house.

When they didn't find what they were looking for, they stayed. For three days they remained, keeping an eye on her and periodically demanding to know where Farzad was hiding. Afsana had no information to give them and knew Farzad was too smart to return with jeeps parked outside and soldiers prowling about. The soldiers helped themselves to the food in the house and what they couldn't stuff into their stomachs, they carelessly wasted.

The fourth day after descending on their home, someone delivered a note. The highest-ranking soldier strode toward her, hands clasped behind his back, a wicked gleam in his eyes. "This has gone on long enough. I will ask you one more time, where is your husband?"

Fear squirmed in Afsana's belly, warning her things were about to change. "I truly do not know."

"Then we have no choice but to arrest you in his stead." He signaled the guard nearest her who grabbed her by the wrist and yanked her to her feet. "We are leaving now. We will trade her for the freedom fighter Farzad Mansour."

Afsana and her mother clung to each other, terrified and wet-faced with tears. When the soldiers dragged her away, her mother wrapped herself around her daughter and wailed.

"Don't take her! Please don't. She just got married, she is so young."

The soldiers pushed her parents to the floor, pointing guns, ready to shoot them.

"No!" her father cried. He leaped to his feet, pleading with them to spare their daughter. "This is all a misunderstanding. If you'd just give me a chance to explain. She is innocent."

He ran forward and tried to free Afsana but one of the soldiers shot him in the leg.

"Abbu! Abbu!" Afsana cried as they dragged her outside and thrust her into a jeep. Horrified, she watched her father dragged from the home and shoved into another jeep, crimson stains spreading over his pant leg.

Afsana gazed mutely out the window, the town she'd grown up in and knew like the back of her hand had now become unfamiliar, swarming with soldiers, tanks, and jeeps. Piles of rubble, forlorn in the morning haze, smoldered, burned-out shells once brimming with life.

The jeep pulled up in front of an internment camp surrounded by barbed wire. Security guards armed with guns kept a watchful eye on the interior of the camp from inside the towers while military police patrolled the external areas. Groups of women prisoners huddled together, watching Afsana join them as the soldiers grabbed her arm and yanked her from the vehicle.

She kept her eyes down as she shuffled past them. She was taken into a small room and shoved into a chair. Several soldiers kept silent guard over her until another joined them. He stood above her, giving her time to wonder what they would do to her, what would become of her.

"Where is your husband?" The whispered words reverberated around the room as powerfully as if he'd shouted.

Sweat trickled down her temple, her heart thudding. She knew she could not give these men what they wanted. And she knew they would never believe her. "I do not know."

One of the soldiers put a gun to her head.

"We've been watching him. He came to see you several nights ago." The simpleness of the words and the quiet way he delivered them scared her more than if he had screamed in her face.

She took a deep breath, the air catching in her throat.

"He left no information of his whereabouts," she replied. Thoughts began to race through her mind. Would she ever see her parents again? Would she leave this room alive?

"What about the others who were with him?"

"I know of no others," Afsana replied, thinking about Nasir and Saif. Had they accompanied Farzad, or had they fled individually? Or had they, too, been captured?

One of the soldiers grabbed her roughly by the shoulder and dragged her from the chair, tossing her into a corner of the room. He threw icy water on her.

Now the interrogator shouted. "Where have they gone!"

"I do not know. I have no information to give you. Please!" She wished Farzad had allowed her to run with him. She could be safely hidden alongside him. Did he not consider that this could happen?

Afsana had never been struck. The backhanded blow across her face took her breath away and left her ears ringing.

The soldier squatted in front of her. "Do you know what we can do to you?" He ran a finger down her throbbing cheek when she did not reply. He yanked her to her feet and shoved her back into the chair. "Anything we want to."

One of the guards grabbed her arms and twisted them behind her, binding her wrists. He kicked the chair out from under her, forcing her to squat. Unable to catch herself, she wobbled, her legs quivering after only a few minutes. The interrogator grabbed her shirt and yanked her to a standing position, pressing his body against her. Her blouse tore, dangling from one shoulder and exposing her breast. With her hands bound behind her, she had no means of gathering the tattered clothing to cover herself.

"*Anything* we want to," he repeated. "And we will, until you answer our questions." He showed her pictures of prominent freedom fighters. "Do you know this man?"

Most of them were students at Dhaka University. Of course she knew them. She'd been in classes with them. But she shook her head again and again, denying any knowledge of them. She certainly had no idea where to find any of them.

She continued shaking her head until he held up a picture of Farzad. He laughed when she stopped, mid-shake, and hung her head.

"You would even deny your own husband? Of course you know this one. And all the others. You will tell us where they are. You will. I promise." He leaned in, snaking an arm around her waist and pulling her quaking body against him. She could feel his arousal through his uniform. "You will give me everything I want."

When he released her, the other two grabbed her and shoved her back into the corner. They threw icy water on her again and continued to backhand her across her face, which throbbed and ached from the beating. She could feel the welts swelling. When they left, she fell against the wall and slid into a sitting position, weeping. *Farzad, why did you leave me here at their mercy?*

She was kept in complete isolation, hands constantly tied behind her back. Her arms and shoulders ached, then throbbed, then went numb. She was deprived of food and sleep until she began to hallucinate. For weeks, the men returned to ask her the same questions she could not answer.

Ten

THE WAR HEROINE

Nafisa was not surprised when Pakistani soldiers arrived at her house. She'd seen and heard about women being picked up and driven away. But she didn't intend to make their job easy for them.

"You cannot do this to me! Tell me why I am being arrested!"

The officer signaled the men to back off. He came to the door and asked her to come out of the house. When she asked the reason once again, he responded, "I'll tell you the reason when we get into the truck."

Nafisa didn't move, meeting his eyes defiantly. He grabbed her by the arm and threw her to two soldiers waiting nearby. They forced her to her knees. She glanced briefly at the officer's shiny boots as she was dragged before him by the two soldiers. One of them gave her a sharp blow to the back of her head. "Stand up straight!"

Dizzy, ears ringing, she complied and was cuffed before being shoved into the small convoy truck. Inside, she joined other women prisoners of different ages standing back-to-back in a line. She did not know who was taking her or where she was being taken. And despite his earlier promise, the officer continued to avoid answering her.

"I am in the truck," she told him. "Where are you taking me? And why?"

"Don't talk so much. If you help me, I will help you." The officer's gaze swept over her body, making her skin crawl. After that, she stopped speaking to him, hoping to avoid any further unwanted attention from the man.

They traveled through the night before the convoy stopped. The soldiers climbed out, stood on the road and ate. They allowed their prisoners to come out for a moment to breathe fresh air in the open country by the side of the road. Nafisa spent her moments outside the truck gauging the soldiers and her surroundings, trying to determine where they were and where they might be headed.

"Please, can I have a glass of water?" The soldiers ignored her first several requests, but eventually one left to find water.

She lowered her head and watched carefully until the other guards, distracted with food and conversation, forgot all about her. She slipped away, racing down a path she'd spotted leading away from the road. She had no idea where it would lead but didn't care. She only wanted to get away and return home. She crashed through the overgrown brush until she stumbled onto a small river a considerable distance from the truck. The trees that fringed the edges of the waterway would act as temporary shelter tonight—and a hiding place for now.

Behind her, she heard the cries of soldiers as they realized what she'd done. "She's gone! She ran away!"

"I'm sure she is hiding somewhere," she heard the officer who had leered at her say. A smack followed his angry words. "I shouldn't have let her out of my sight, not even for a second. You soldiers are worthless!"

She heard them crashing through the brush, searching for her. Heart hammering, she left her hiding place behind, picking her way to the edge of the water.

"There she is! I've found her!"

Nafisa turned to see the other soldiers joining the one who

had spotted her. She jumped into the river. A good swimmer, she might have been able to escape but was fatigued from lack of food and sleep. She lagged and floundered against the current and ran out of breath as she fought to put distance between herself and the soldiers.

They caught up with her, dragged her from the water, tied her wrists together with rope, and took her back to the waiting truck. Nafisa offered no resistance this time. She would be quiet and cooperative until they trusted her again and perhaps let their guard down. Even though she tried not to be noticed, the officer kept his eyes on her. He seemed amused or perhaps in some way taken with her. Every time she chanced a glance, those dark eyes of his still drank her in.

The truck bumped along, continuing the trek toward whatever fate held in store for her. She lost track of time completely before it groaned to a halt.

The doors of the convoy were opened.

"You can all come out," the officer announced.

Nafisa followed the line of women and soon they were in a courtyard of sorts, surrounded by a wall. Of the two adjacent buildings, one had the appearance of a barrack and the other, with bars at all the windows, looked more like a prison.

The sun had already set by the time Nafisa arrived at the barracks. She stretched her legs and craned her neck as the soldiers demanded the women follow them. All was tranquil and reposed, save the mournful cry of birds of prey in the far distance. She looked up at the sky to discover that it was not a moonless night. And the rising moon, like a timid, blushing nymph, rose from the silvery clouds to take on an eerie silver glow, when its rays broke through the darkness. With its thickly studded stars, the sky looked on calmly, as if nothing unusual was going on beneath them.

A man dressed in a faded uniform was seated at a table, pen in hand, writing down the names of the prisoners as they disembarked from the truck.

When it was Nafisa's turn, the man asked her name.

"I'm not in a mood to tell you my name. Where are we?" she asked.

"You are in Khulna," he replied. "And I suggest you provide your name if you know what is good for you."

The soldiers led them separately, each to their allotted room. Nafisa was escorted by the soldier who had fished her from the river, his uniform still damp. He squeezed her arm harder than necessary and threw her into the cell. He slammed the door, and she heard the bolt shot from outside.

Some time later, she awoke to somebody unbolting her door and there stood the officer with a guard.

The officer eyed her as she sat up on her cot. He dismissed the guard. "You may go. See that I am not disturbed."

Nafisa shrank against the wall, far more frightened than she had been since her arrest.

"It's no use running away from me. Where will you go? You and I are going to be together from now on." The officer kept his voice low. He approached her the way a hungry tiger advances toward its prey, slow and calculating, his face flushed with suppressed excitement.

He even smiled at her as he sat down and crossed his legs in an indifferent sort of way, like an indolent man, thoroughly satisfied with himself and the whole world. But his small, greedy eyes gave him away as they sparkled with lust, drinking her in.

He stared at the round, unleavened bread on her plate.

"Why haven't you eaten your food?" he demanded.

Nafisa met his eyes but did not respond.

"You are not hungry?" he asked, placing emphasis on the last word, conveying his own appetite.

She shook her head and twisted her hands, but the rope would not come loose. Her breath came in jagged gasps as she worked her wrists until the rope rubbed her skin raw.

But it still held fast.

"Does that hurt you?" he asked, moving to sit next to her.

"These foolish soldiers tied your bonds so tight. Look, you're bleeding." He dragged a finger over her arm. "Will you be nice to me if I free you?"

Nafisa dropped her eyes and shook her head, recoiling from his touch.

He laughed lightly. "I will free you anyway, and soon you will calm down and start learning to love me." He seized his knife and with a few strokes severed the rope that bound her hands.

"Please let me go," she whispered. "Let me go home."

"I cannot do that. You may as well make the best of your current situation. I can ensure you receive more food. I can protect you from the other guards."

"I am not hungry," she answered.

Straightening up suddenly, the officer's tone became stern.

"I can also ensure you receive no food. Or allow the guards into your cell at their will. They are already enjoying the other women. All I want is to protect you." He spat on the ground.

"Protect me? You've kidnapped me from my parents' house, and to what end? How is that protecting me?"

The officer smirked. "I only followed orders. But now that we are here, why not make the best of the situation?" His eyes darkened and blazed with an intensity that terrified her. His face flushed, twitched with impatience. Lashing out, he grabbed her wrist and yanked her into him, held her, forced her head back. The strength of his purpose was expressed in his powerful grip.

There was nothing else she could do. Nafisa neither answered nor moved but gazed at him in helpless terror.

Was it the world around her that started fading or was it her eyes that were blurring her view? She could not tell. She closed her eyes tightly, tears leaking from the corners.

"Please don't do this," she whispered. "Please."

Her soft pleas, which grew softer the more terrified she became, seemed only to feed his frenzy. He seized her by the shoulders, then curled one arm around her waist and tugged her against his groin. The heat of shame rushed to her face.

He snaked his other hand into her hair, behind her head, and pulled her face to his.

As his stale breath blew against her and his lips found her neck, the young, handsome face of Saif flashed before her eyes, sitting between his parents at her home in Dhaka. He had refused to shift his eyes from her gaze as they spoke of his accomplishments to her family.

Nafisa had known by looking into his face that Saif did not care what his parents were saying. She was absolutely sure that he had stopped listening to a word of what was being exchanged between the families the moment he had one look at Nafisa. She had seen, too, that he had already known in his mind that it was her, and her alone, that he would consecrate his life to, whose hands he would hold till death did they part. And she, unable to withdraw her gaze from him, felt a frisson of happiness as their parents shook hands and embraced.

Rough hands clawed at the waistband of her britches, pulling Nafisa's thoughts from the best moment of her life to this, the worst. The moment would change everything, destroying the future she had so happily daydreamed of. No longer in control, she held her breath as the officer lowered her to the ground, resting his body on her to hold her in place as he fumbled with his pants. Her eyes were closed, her lips were sealed. She disconnected from the act, as his fingers moved against her as blades, carving memories into her flesh that would leave scars long past being healed.

Barely able to breathe, Nafisa stared in despair at the engagement ring Saif had given her not too long ago. This truly was the end of all things, and she was faced with a life where the laws of nature had been broken.

Eleven

THE ESCAPE

Nasir moved cautiously in the direction of the Pakistani camp. He hoped to find his sister in one of the notorious army barracks. A sense of approaching danger alerted him. He froze, tempted to shoot at the slightest provocation but waiting to see if he was attacked first. After what seemed rather an endless length of time, the shuffling of heavy boots moved beyond his hiding place.

When he started again toward the camp, it was getting close to midnight and the darkness engulfed him completely. Not a bit of light cracked the blackness of the moonless night. No shimmering stars illuminated the sky. The entire world seemed to hold its breath, waiting to see if he would be caught. He crept closer and closer in total obscurity until he was in the very heart of the enemy stronghold. A place where it was easier to get into than out of, he was aware that he was risking his life with every step he took and the chances were that he might never come back alive. He listened, always straining to hear the cracking of a dry bough or any sound that might come from within. But there was none.

His foot hit the crouching form of a guard. The sleepy man woke and gripped his ankle, but Nasir wrenched himself free.

His experience in the army and as a freedom fighter had prepared him for combat.

For a few minutes their weapons did not come of any use. In an instant they were rolling and tumbling in the dirt, and for the space of a minute, they tugged and tore at each other's hair and clothes, punching and scratching each other like enemies in their last agony in the same battlefield. But not for long. They toppled over, landed with a thud. Nasir saw the gleam of a dagger in his enemy's hand. He let the soldier come close to him, slapped the arm that held the knife, and knocked it out of his hand. Nasir pounced on the weapon, afraid to fire his gun for fear of detection. A well-placed dagger ended a man's life just as well as a bullet.

Panting with exertion, he stood over his victim, ready to stab him again if he moved. Having overcome his antagonist, he found himself in a narrow passageway. He groped around and stood still for a moment to allow his eyes to adjust to the pitch-dark passages. Nasir crept cautiously toward the door, then stood still for a moment.

He waited as it creaked on its hinges. Someone, hardly recognizable in the dark, appeared before him. It was the caretaker whom he had bribed the previous night for information about Nafisa's whereabouts. The man had not given him much, but he'd confirmed he had seen Nafisa.

"But you'll never make it inside to rescue her," he'd said. "Do not risk your life."

Now, seeing Nasir inside the barracks, the caretaker's eyes widened.

Nasir grabbed the man by his shoulders. "Please. Tell me where my sister is. She is so young. I only want to save her."

The caretaker covered his face with his hands. "Forgive me. I did not think you would truly come to rescue her. I should have told you yesterday. Your sister was found to be pregnant—"

"Pregnant!"

"—and was freed. She is no longer here. But she is alive."

"Or she was, when you sent her out into the world pregnant and alone with no support." Nasir covered his face with the back of his hands and wept helplessly. "I should have stayed back at home and protected her. She is my only sister and is engaged to be married, but now look at her fate! Even if she is alive, who will marry her? No one will take her for their wife carrying another man's child."

Nasir let go of the caretaker, thanking him.

He would continue his search, find Nafisa, bring her home—

As he turned to leave, he saw a dim light streaming underneath a door. Something drew him closer. From inside, he heard a raspy cough and realized the room was occupied. His fingers tightened upon the small pistol he carried in his right hand. The door seemed unlocked as he gently pushed it open, just a crack. His beloved sister Nafisa could be a prisoner in this room, he thought. What if the caretaker had been mistaken? As he took a couple more steps, he heard a rustling. The dim light in the small room provided a faint outline of fixtures and furniture. A lantern stood on a dusty table, but there were no chairs in the room.

He noticed a single bed against the wall. He muttered an apology, at a person who sat leaning against the wall with legs drawn up to their chest, face partially covered with a veil, hands tightly clasped around the knees.

"Nafisa?" he asked, as he stepped out of the shadows, desperate for the form to belong to his sister.

The woman lifted her veil and peered at him. "Nasir?"

Then her face relaxed and her eyes seemed to sparkle ever so slightly despite the dullness of the room.

Nasir's heart sank at the sight of his comrade Farzad's wife. His quick glance at her sorry state, her haggard, emaciated looks, her disheveled hair, torn clothes, told him everything.

"What are you doing here? You shouldn't be here, Nasir. Do you realize how dangerous it is to be in the enemy barracks? You need to get out of here."

"I came to find Nafisa. Are you alone? How long have you been a prisoner?"

"I don't even know. It seems so long, and I wonder when I will see the sun again."

"Come with me. I will take you from here, and you can breathe fresh air again, if only you'll do what I tell you to do."

An intense fear engulfed her. "Where is Farzad? Do you know?"

"No, I don't know where he is. He has disappeared. He is either captured, or he is hiding somewhere. I didn't know that you were one of those unfortunate women brought here to be tortured by the army. If not Nafisa, at least I found you. I'm not leaving without you." Nasir looked at Afsana encouragingly. "But you must come at once. We'll start while the camp sleeps. I've already killed one guard, and if we encounter another, I'll kill him too. Your escape will not be known until the break of dawn."

What she saw in Nasir's face evidently assured her. Her eyes lit up with a new joy, a new wild hope. He saw her amazement, the incredulity in her eyes at the possibility of escape from the terrible situation she was in.

"You need a disguise. Here." He handed her a wrapped package.

She pulled the paper away, revealing a man's loose shirt and a pair of pants he'd intended to hand over to Nafisa. At least they would serve to rescue someone.

"Give me a moment." She hurriedly changed into her male disguise, pulled back her hair into a messy low bun, tucked it in, and covered it with a white scarf.

Nasir looked at her with an approving glance. "You can pass as a young man, except for the fact that your face appears too fine and delicate. Perhaps a young boy," he remarked with a soft chuckle.

He led her back the way he'd entered, retracing his steps, barely breathing for fear of discovery. They stepped carefully around the body of the guard he'd dispatched, thankfully still undiscovered.

At the end of the hallway, Nasir hunkered down against the wall, his eyes squeezed shut. He held an arm out to halt Afsana. He listened intently. If they were caught, it would be the death of them both. Afsana would look to him to lead her to safety, when he had no idea where they would go.

He made up his mind and stood. "It's a long walk, but we have to make it, Afsana." He had failed his sister, but he would make it right. He would ensure someone left this camp safely tonight. He stepped out into the night, Afsana close behind.

As they crept through the darkness, the muffled noise of repeated gunshots reverberated in the air. The sound startled away the early morning birds perched on the branches. An owl screeched from somewhere in the trees. Was it crying a warning? Or alerting the soldiers to their escape?

Nasir shivered.

The booming of artillery and gunfire resonated in the distance. The glow of raging fires lit up the sky. As they traveled through the night, the roads became more dangerous, but Nasir knew them like the palm of his hand from his work as a freedom fighter.

He fell, stumbled, and clawed his way through the thick jute trees and soon found himself in a dense forest, pulling Afsana along with him. Exhausted, Nasir became concerned about his companion, who he could see needed to take rest. He led her to the base of a tree and leaned her against it. She breathed heavily but made no complaint as he offered some food from a small cloth bag he carried.

When the stars winked from the sky, they gathered their belongings and started to walk again, pressing through the thick trees and overgrown brush. While scrambling halfway up a rubble-strewn slope, the report of a rifle boomed, and the noise echoed out into the forest's silence. Off and on, the hazy sky was illuminated with several quick, bright-red flashes, again and again. A flash went off in front of and perhaps a hundred yards beneath them, then another and another as battery after battery of anti-aircraft guns came into action to form a barrage around the area. Nasir found himself in the midst of a crossfire, and death was perhaps the only absolute certainty if they were to cross through that deluge of shells.

Bullets whizzed around them, smacked on the ground, and burst on all sides of them. As they stared, a blue spurt of smoke issued, followed by the roar of another shot that whisked past them in a puff of wind. A whirring followed by a whizzing—a bullet just missed his ear and sang over Nasir's head. He feared that the next bullet might strike him or Afsana. He dashed behind a huge rock and sat her down. He slipped over a heap of rocks and fell headlong, sprawling in the pebbles.

He sat still, staring into the sky as the world crashed around him. The noise was deafening in his ears. With a moan, he covered his face with his hands, unable to see a way out of this.

Pain radiated up his arm. Blood on his fingers confirmed he was hit this time. He cursed his fate, unable to raise his elbow.

Blood soaked the sleeve of his shirt.

He sat up unsteadily and turned to look in his companion's direction. He saw her head flop back, not stirring as she lay quite still with her eyes closed. Had Afsana been hit too? Choking back his fear, he crawled to her and tried to raise her head.

"Are you badly hurt?" he asked.

To his great relief, she came around and shook her head. Her wide eyes and silence seemed to indicate she was shell shocked. But being dazed and scared was better than being shot.

Spread over and above them, the open, endless night sky offered no shelter, no comfort. Had he been alone, Nasir might have succumbed to the empty loneliness that split his chest, an aching punctuated by the relentless rattling gunfire and booming blasts that pierced the darkness.

And yet he was not alone. Conscious of each muscle of his feet on the ground, a new fear seized him—fear for Afsana's safety. In the distance, acres of dense shadowy woods, tall jute trees, and small ravines surrounded them, providing natural protection from the fight. If they could just make it a little farther, they could take cover there.

And at that moment, out in the dead of the night, thinking of the long journey that lay behind him and the great stretch before him, the soft breathing sound of another living soul brought an unexpected comfort to him.

"Are you all right, Afsana? How are you feeling?"

Again, she spoke no words, merely nodded mutely in response.

"Come," he said and held out his hand to help her to her feet. Now that he had a plan, he was impatient to move again.

As he pulled her up, she stumbled slightly. He caught her instantly when she fell against him.

"You need to rest," he said, releasing her. "We'll start again after you've had some sleep."

She looked up briefly. "I can't. I can't walk anymore. I feel all right when I lie still, but when I get up, the blood rushes to my head and I feel dizzy and lightheaded. I'm not going to make it, Nasir."

Afsana sat down and covered her face with her hands. She began to cry mournfully and unceasingly as if everything wasn't the way it should be. "You must regret rescuing me now."

"Not in the least," he said.

"It looks like my injuries are worse than they appear." She rubbed her ankle and grimaced in pain. "It's my ankle. I think I sprained it on the rocks where I fell."

He bent low, trying to ascertain the extent of her injury by the light of the moon.

"Oh, Nasir, you are bleeding!" she cried, noticing blood on the sleeve of his shirt. "Maybe we should look for shelter where we can rest and tend to your wounds."

"A bullet grazed my arm. It looks worse than it is," he said. "I will be fine. And you will make it. We are not very far from the border."

Though he spoke encouragingly to Afsana, Nasir wondered if he could, in fact, see them safely across the border. The border was too daunting a goal, so he set his sights on finding someplace to wait out the battle currently raging around them.

He pulled Afsana to her feet. Leaning on one another, she limped along beside him, propping up his wounded arm. Eventually, they made the shelter of the grove, collapsed into the shadows of the dense trees, completely exhausted, and settled into the dirt to sleep.

When they woke, the silence of the breaking dawn signaled a lapse in fighting. Afsana's ankle had swollen horribly, the skin black and blue, but his arm had stopped bleeding. He fashioned a walking stick for her out of a fallen branch—a poor substitute for medical attention but better than nothing.

Sticking to the relative safety of wooded areas, they continued their trek, stopping regularly when the heat became unbearable or when Afsana simply could not move another step. He managed to find water in streams but no food. After several days of grumbling angrily, his stomach gave up complaining.

The journey seemed endless, and yet finally, after five days of hobbled travel, completely exhausted and in great pain, they found themselves in a paddy field. Across the fields, perhaps a mile away, to their great relief and much surprise, they came across a cluster of bamboo-hut-style homesteads dotting the flat plain. Some of them had thatched roofs and some had corrugated metal roofs. Nearby they saw fruit-bearing trees and a pond. Nasir eyed the pond ravenously, eager for the source of water that would provide for drinking, bathing, laundry, and fish.

But the silence and the lone homes shocked him. He was disheartened to see the absence of smoke billowing from these bamboo huts, a common feature in a rural setting.

Nasir stood still, listening so hard his ears strained from the effort. He heard nothing, not even the comforting sounds of wildlife going about their business, assuring them they had nothing to fear. They approached warily, Nasir torn between hoping one of these huts would offer empty refuge, and the hope he had found help. If only he could be sure anyone inside would be friendly to them, he would know how to proceed.

A red brick structure had a veranda in the front, with an inviting little walkway leading up to the house. The house looked neglected, as if the earth was ready to reclaim it, to take it back into its arms. The twittering of birds on the nearby trees was the only sound pervading the scene of desolation. And remembering that the light would not last long, both Nasir and Afsana followed the dry, leaf-strewn path to the front door. The small windows of the house were shut and refused to allow the sunlight inside. The door was closed too. Wind and rain had whipped a coating of gritty dust against the panels and deep into the crack where the door opened, proving that it had not been opened for quite some time. When Nasir tried to open the door, it yielded easily.

It was pitch dark inside. Darting beams of his flashlight barely illuminated the next few feet of inky darkness. Nasir took Afsana by the hand and led her into the rooms slowly and hesitantly. When their eyes adjusted to the utter darkness, they noticed that spiders had created an irregular network of webs in the corners and on the ceiling of the room.

The house, with little interior decoration, used to be home to a real family. Black and white photos of the former home-owners gave off a tragic, deathly sense and filled Nasir with a poignant longing for home, for family. It surely contained the dusty remnants of life mysteriously interrupted. The uncanny mix of normality and weirdness of the house made Nasir's skin crawl, the otherworldly atmosphere a bizarre imitation of home.

Scattered teacups with residual stains on a low, well-worn table caught their attention. The people who lived here had failed to wash them in their urgency. Clothes were still hanging up to dry, food remained stored in the kitchen. Tall trees shook their fruits into the yard, but they lay untouched. Time seemed to have stopped in this dismal house, a creepy memory of another life. Everything remained as it was, as if the owners just disappeared one day. The bleak emptiness of the house sent a shudder through Afsana. Nasir wrapped his arms around her gently.

Nasir sent Afsana into the kitchen to check for any supplies and went into the woods to gather firewood.

When he returned, Nasir discovered Afsana had gathered small sticks for kindling and already had a little fire started. She had found a metal pot and was boiling water. She poured it into a bowl and with a clean, soft piece of cloth she cleaned his wounds. She mixed some of the sterilized water with turmeric she found in the pantry of the abandoned home. She formed a turmeric paste and applied it to his abrasions to fight off infection. The paste was supposed to act as an antiseptic.

For a brief moment, he allowed himself to relax.

"You'll come to like this place in the morning," he assured her. "Maybe we'll rest and stay for a couple of days and survive on fruits from the trees and water in the pond."

Once Afsana had completed tending to his wounds, Nasir stood on the veranda and listened intently, feeling as if all around him things buzzed with more life than during the day. The luscious green fields turned into a strange and eerie landscape, whispering . . . warnings? Or murmurs of solace? Centuries-old trees surrounded them with sprawling limbs, gaunt and somber, having kept guard over the land and everything that transpired. The deep forest was ancient. Nothing surprised it anymore. The mystery of the great forest exercised a spell peculiarly of its own. The sense of unfamiliarity grew upon Nasir as he stood there watching. The loneliness of the place had entered into his very bones, and silence seemed natural, for after a bit the sound of his own and that of Afsana's voice became a trifle unreal and forced, until whispering became their form of communication.

The woodland trees, rivers, and streams tingled with life,

stirred up and awakened abruptly. They transformed into living things. The lonely but melodious note of a hooting owl perched on the huge *neem* tree frightened him, just the way the *neem* tree in the backyard of his childhood home had beckoned him in the middle of the night during his youth. The owl's eyes seemed to penetrate deep into his innermost thoughts. He ran to the bottom of the tree on which it had perched, but it was not there, nor did he hear any sound of beating wings. It had disappeared into the shadows.

He could not see the river at night, but he could hear it racing down from the hills, over trunks and boulders. All the other sounds were lost in the noise of its splashing and eddying against the green and slimy banks. He heard it talking, burbling around rocks, whispering its soothing words of wisdom. The steady murmur could easily lull him to sleep. He half-closed his eyes, listening to its rippling noises. It was hard to believe that the same river, a roaring terror of swift water during the day, could change so abruptly.

The whispering breezes came rustling through the quivering leaves, moaning and puffing in the dark. Leaves began to fold and unfold. The wind was high, and the somber trees stirred and shifted. Their boughs rubbed against each other, producing unearthly groans and creaks. During the day, they had been silent, but awoke to prattle on softly at night, in tones scarcely human, an unintelligible language.

Nasir wondered if the night made things seem spookier. Or was it merely a trick of the mind? Were these illusory experiences a manifestation of his agitated brain, perhaps his over-wrought nerves? Or the misty influence of the atmosphere? He began to feel as though he were under a spell.

For an undaunted person like Nasir, the entire experience proved a little too eerie for comfort.

"Do these trees come alive at night? Perhaps they hide themselves during the day, only to fully reveal themselves when the moon rises." His thoughts ran on randomly.

As a *Mukti Joddha*, he was always alert to unusual sounds or noise. The snapping of a twig in his path or a distant step on leaves would immediately send messages to his brain to be cautious and to be on guard.

Still, it was unnaturally peaceful and quiet. It was all too quiet.

Nature seemed to remain unconcerned and heedless to the threats of the roaring guns that Afsana and Nasir had escaped, replacing it with droning background music of chirping crickets and croaking frogs, a symphony of courtship song filling the night air.

This symphony was broken at long intervals by the wail of a weary night bird's sad calling, too frightened to settle on the branches. With a shudder, Nasir went back inside.

"I think we're safe," he reassured Afsana. "We will be able to rest and recover nicely here."

Twelve

THE MARTYR

The next day, at the break of dawn, soft sunrays reached into the sky. A white morning haze hung, stretching over the green fields, dusting them in a silvery-golden luster. The air outside was heavy, laden with the sweet aroma of a short-stem variety of rice from the paddy fields mingled with a faint scent of an unknown flower. The swaying reeds of grass along the rice fields rippled to the rhythm of the breeze. Nearby fields of mustard and sweet peas bobbed and nodded along.

The light of day dispelled the eeriness of the previous night. The abandoned home proved to be a safe place for them to rest and recover. To their great relief, they spotted a portable hurricane lantern in one corner of the house. It had a large glass globe with a heavier metal base and a fully adjustable wick to illuminate a larger area.

Afsana and Nasir were overjoyed to find cool drinking water in an earthen water pot in the kitchen. After days of parched travel, they finally quenched their thirst. They found some stored rice and lentils and flour. Before long, Afsana had prepared a whole-wheat flat bread and some rice and *daal*. They even used water from the pond to freshen up.

By their second night, the abandoned house began to feel

like home. Just when they made themselves comfortable, Nasir thought he heard a noise outside. It sounded like faint shuffling steps occurring at regular intervals, as if someone was walking and resting.

A moment later, it turned into the sound of something being dragged along the path. Afsana began to look around, wide-eyed and alert.

Nasir gathered his courage and went out the door to investigate. Someone had collapsed, lying face down. He crept closer, his nerves on edge, and discovered that it was a wounded soldier, bleeding profusely from his lacerated legs. Nasir considered it a miracle that the man had managed to drag himself this far.

He gazed intently at the prostrated figure, still alive but barely breathing. Taking his flashlight out, he shone it on the soldier's face and, with a jolt, fell back as he recognized the fallen freedom fighter. The handsome face, so young, had a high pale forehead, his damp, dark hair brushed away, the lips pale and bloodless. The weary eyes peered up at Nasir. A quivering smile of recognition spread on the soldier's face when he found Nasir's eyes fixed on him, a sweet calmness settling over him.

"It's Saif," he called to Afsana, peering at him from the door.

"Nafisa's betrothed?"

"Indeed."

Afsana scurried to join him, her little feet soft on the ground. The crescent moon shot a pallid gleam across Nasir and Afsana, where, like ghosts, they crouched around Saif's prone form. The lurking shadow of death lurched toward this freedom fighter. The clouds, filled with shame, seemed to wrap around them, as if to ensure the moon's glow would not witness the horror of that night.

The cool breeze touched his face, making it look more sublime, but he did not seem to be in pain. Saif's life was ebbing away. Death stood nearby, and its gray shadow fell across the young soldier. Nasir sat back on his heels and placed Saif's head on his lap, tears flowing copiously down his cheeks as he noticed a composed languor in his expression. He gave vent to his grief and decided to remain at his side until the end, bearing witness as Saif crossed from this world to the next, a journey no one should make alone. Afsana gazed at this brave young heart who faced all the circumstances of the times in which he lived. She too slowly knelt beside their fallen friend.

With the break of dawn, a dove from the rooftop of the house cooed its forlorn yet soothing call, as if to assist Saif in seeking and finding inner peace.

Saif looked up with his surrendering eyes. "Please tell my mother that I've died happily and died in honor. It is good to die for our country. Tell her to be kind to Nafisa, whose face I shall never see again." He reached for Nasir's hand and squeezed it. "*Joy Bangla.*"

As Nasir felt Saif's hand go limp, he repeated, "*Joy Bangla.*"

The flashlight fell from his hands, smeared with Saif's blood. He stroked the young man's hair. He didn't know that Saif had joined the liberation army. He remembered him as a young lad who always had lofty dreams, always immersed in contemporary Bengali literature and writing poetry. He came from a very well-to-do family. So many times, he thought of him as a perfect groom for his younger sister—someone who would care for her and appreciate her.

"You are a gallant soldier, Saif. Hold on. We will get help for you. I'm sure Nafisa will be so proud of you someday when you both see each other again," Nasir whispered into his ear.

"It would have been better for him if he had never been born," Afsana remarked. "Better for all of us if we had never been born."

Nasir smiled despairingly at her remark. "The strange thing is that we are all going to die someday. We worry and let ourselves suffer. When we are dead, will it matter at all? What difference will it make? And yet we are here and fighting to make a difference for the lives you are so quick to wish away. If we could get some medical attention for him, I think he could pull through. Regardless, we can't leave him behind."

Before they could decide what to do, a deep, gruff voice called out, breaking the silence of the night.

"It looks like we have more visitors," Nasir remarked.

Two individuals appeared from nowhere. Their well-built and still-strong bodies were visible through their torn and tattered clothing. No doubt these two men had fought the enemy at close range. The musky odor of sweat and death emanated from their bodies.

Nasir stood, relieved to see the brothers. He recognized the twins he had fought beside. "You seem to be ready to go home. Did you ever do anything besides blow up bridges?"

"During the day, we built roads and strips for helicopters to land on. Unfortunately, we were not equipped with enough explosives, so some days we could only destroy part of the bridges, and only part of them would collapse."

"But even then, it was enough to disrupt the movement of Pakistani forces," the other twin remarked. "I was in charge of getting equipment to and from the frontline, and some days we both fought side by side."

"And I also cleared landmines and built bridges. We were clearing a minefield when one of the engineers stepped on one and tripped the wire. It blew up, and four of my men were injured. One died on the spot and another lost his leg."

"The war will end soon. It's only a matter of time before those confounded Pakistanis surrender," one of them confided.

"Well, if that's the case, could you take care of Saif? He needs immediate medical attention. I am taking Afsana with me to the border." He gestured to her standing nearby. "This house is empty, if you'd like to join us."

"Sure, we'll take Saif inside the house. We'll make him comfortable till we can get him to the hospital."

But it was not to be. When the morning star grew pale in the green sky, Saif succumbed to his wounds and breathed his last, before Nasir and Afsana left for the final leg of their journey.

~

Afsana had grown comfortable traveling with Nasir and knew she could trust him. Fear gripped her heart when they encountered a couple of approaching Indian border patrolmen. Nasir waved to them and confirmed they were helping displaced people take refuge in the camps on the Indian side of the border.

"You must go with them," Nasir encouraged her.

"Life is not going to be easy for you here in the camps," one of the guards remarked.

"I think he'll be fine," Nasir replied, trying to pass Afsana off as a young male soldier.

The Indian soldier was not so easily convinced and moved closer to Afsana, scrutinizing her face. She could smell his body odor as he leaned close. She kept her eyes down, but he snatched her head cover off before she knew what was happening, unveiling her face.

"You're not a boy. You must be one of the young women rescued from the army barracks. You can join the other women." He led her to a huddled group.

Nasir remained by her side, as if he too was hesitant to end their journey together.

"Thank you for getting me out of the clutches of the army, Nasir," Afsana said. "I want to start all over again by moving to a place where nobody will know me. I left my home, my relatives. I have no one to go back to. You have family, and I'm sure you'll find Nafisa. She needs your love and support."

"As far as I am concerned, I am staying in Dhaka. There is so much to do now that we are a free country. And you are right, Afsana. I'll find my sister first."

Bruised and alone, Afsana turned to the guards, determined to start a new chapter of her life. But life at the crowded camps was like nothing she had experienced before. The simple shelters were little more than huts made of bamboo sticks with plastic sheeting for walls and tarpaulins overhead.

The individual rooms were small, and everyone shared one communal bathroom, where women could bathe only twice a week. The camp suffered a scarcity of toilets as well. She walked a long way and stood in line when she needed to use the facilities, including when it was her turn to take a cold bucket bath. She fetched water from the communal tap in the camp to drink, cook with, and clean with. And for that she made the trip an average of three times a day.

While grateful that India welcomed refugees, clearly the influx of people was more than they could handle. Thinking back to the home she'd grown up in and the house she'd briefly shared with Farzad, she marveled at the huge upheaval. *I never would have imagined I'd be walking and standing in line to fill a bucket with water just to survive.* Her heart broke whenever she thought of Farzad, who had surely perished in the fighting. She wondered if he, like Saif, had found someone to comfort him in his final moments. She could not breathe at the thought of the loss and decided not to think about it for the time being.

When morning came, Afsana would put away the mattress and blankets so that she could have space in the tent during the day. She opened the flap of her tent and emerged to walk fifteen minutes to the distribution center. She then waited another twenty minutes to get through the line with others. This daily walk was a must to get a small portion of rice and other commodities.

She marveled at how quickly she adapted. Life in the camp became normal. For cooking, she made a small *chula* (cooking fireplace) where she cooked whatever rations she was given. Walking, waiting in line, collecting her rations, bathing, using the toilets—these basic things she'd taken for granted now took all her efforts. She gathered wood from nearby areas to use in her *chula*. But as the weeks passed, and every other refugee sought wood to cook with as well, she walked farther and farther away and returned with less and less wood.

Rice was a staple food. However, with the start of the monsoon season, the heavy rains caused delays in the food deliveries. Portions distributed to the refugees grew smaller and smaller. Rice ran out.

Afsana knew something had to change. She could not live forever in a refugee camp. None of them could. They would eventually run out of food and firewood. Besides, this was no life. She needed to decide what her future would be and leave this behind.

And then everything took an unexpected turn, and she stumbled onto the change she needed when she met Shiraj.

Thirteen

THE CAMP DOCTOR

One bright morning, Shiraj, one of the camp doctors, went on with his usual rounds to treat patients coming in with injuries sustained from the raging war. This was a hastily created make-shift hospital within a refugee camp, not well-equipped to meet the needs of the injured. He was sympathetic to their many hardships as he made his rounds, doing what he could, well aware that what he could offer was a drop in the bucket compared to what they needed. But he had to help as much as he could. The suffering of others cut him deeply.

He walked up to a soldier who sat slumped on the ground for lack of space. As he bent down to wrap a gauze bandage around his head, his attention was drawn toward a patient occupying one of the string beds. She was wearing shabby loose pants and a loose cotton shirt, both in need of washing. Only the dainty nose ring adorning her face proved that she was married, and most likely had seen better days and had a decent life. He studied her face, searching for some clue as to her identity. There was something strangely familiar about the newly arrived patient, her restless brown eyes glancing around the camp and then locking back onto her hands clasped in her lap. So thin. She was so thin and seemed so frail. But no, he could see strength and resolve in those eyes as they glanced about yet again—and found him staring at her. He finished bandaging the soldier and went to the woman's side.

"Please excuse me. Do you mind if I ask you something?" Shiraj swallowed and shifted nervously on his feet, completely unsure as to what to say next. "You must be thinking it's strange that I stare at you so."

"No. Nothing seems strange to me anymore. Not after the things I've seen."

"You seem somehow familiar to me. Is it possible that you are Afsana?"

"Yes." She looked at him carefully. Recognition dawned in her eyes. "And you are Shiraj if I'm not wrong. How nice to meet a friendly face."

Her eyes sparkled in the excitement of realizing she had encountered a familiar person. Her face flushed. Despite her surroundings, he welcomed the sight of her and the long, black, curly hair, which hung loosely around her face. In truth, he had harbored quite a crush on her in their younger days, before she left for university and he for medical school.

"Afsana," he said mournfully, "is this the way we were destined to meet again?"

"Yes, this is how we meet again, unfortunately." Though her face held sorrow, he found warmth and comfort in her voice.

"I'm so sorry you had to go through this. You need time to recuperate. Where is your husband?" he asked.

"I don't know. I have not heard from him since the day he left the house during the early part of the war. I came to know from Nasir, his friend, that nobody knows Farzad's whereabouts. He is either captured or perished in the war."

Shiraj could not bring himself to say a word. His heart stirred at this news of Farzad.

"How do you know Nasir?"

"I knew him from my college days. His sister Nafisa is my

best friend. Nasir went to enemy camps looking for his sister in order to rescue her. He didn't find her. Instead, he found and saved me. And brought me here to the refugee camp."

"What will you do next?" he asked.

"I do not know. I think I am a war widow. What is left for me back in Dhaka but terrible memories? Even the good memories have been overshadowed by the horrible things that happened."

Her words tugged at his heart. He stepped forward and gently took her hand in his. "I will see if I can learn any news about Farzad, if you let me."

Her eyes watered, but she offered him a smile. "I would like that. Thank you."

He realized in that moment that he would do anything for this woman. "For now, let me check on you and your health."

She described twisting her ankle during her escape. "It has never fully healed. I still have a limp."

He lifted her foot, so delicate and precious, and felt gently of the bones and ligaments. "Sprains can take some time to heal. Thankfully, I don't detect anything broken. Let me give you a quick checkup."

Truly, he wanted more time with her. But as camp doctor, he oversaw the general health of the refugees. Gently as possible, he checked her lymph nodes, her throat, and her ears. He placed his stethoscope into his ears and listened to her lungs, first on her chest, then her back. When he placed the stethoscope on her abdomen, he made a startling discovery.

He met her gaze—and saw shame and sadness there.

"Did Farzad know?"

Shiraj noticed that she hesitated to answer. She turned her face away from him.

He sighed deeply. "I understand you may struggle with the decision of whether or not to carry through when you are without a husband."

She stared into her lap and nodded.

"Whatever you decide, I will support you." He considered telling her of the feelings he had once harbored for her, feelings stirring again in her presence.

"Of course you will," she answered faintly. "I remember you. When we were young, you were always a caring person, trying to make others happy. I can tell nothing has changed."

Nothing had changed in his heart, that much he knew. In a bold move, he took her small hand in his own, stroking the back of it with his thumb. When she did not pull her hand away, his heart began to race.

Anxiety gripped him. How could he not be anxious as he realized fate had offered him a second chance at love with his first crush? He had considered her long gone. Only those who fell in love knew the sudden upturn of the world. And in times of war, love could blaze from a tiny spark to a full flame with astonishing speed. From now onwards, she was all in all to him—his life, his soul, his everything.

He bent over and grasped both her hands in his.

"If you will have me, we'll never part, and nothing shall come between us," he assured her. His heart beat so hard in his chest that his entire body shook.

"Oh, Shiraj, you say that because you pity me. You would never have said it otherwise."

"I say it because I love you. I would never have said it otherwise," he answered.

"How could you love me at this moment? Look at me. Look at my predicament. What will people say when my belly swells and I have no husband?"

"Afsana, I loved you many years ago, and I love you still. If you wish to keep this child, I will care for you both. Calm yourself, stay strong for us, and pay no heed to what people may say. It will be no one's business but ours. How beautiful the future will be for both of us. I'm not ashamed to make you mine for as long as I live."

"You will think better about it and change your mind. And I

will not hold it against you. Be sensible, Shiraj. With so many troubles facing us, love is the furthest concern."

"You can tell me all your troubles, whatever they are. I'll take my share and we will face those troubles together. God spared your life and blessed you with a new one. Let's count our blessings."

The next day, Shiraj came to check on her. Joy possessed his soul as he looked upon her once more. He became even more convinced that fate had sent her to him and that it was right, it was inevitable, that he should at least try to win this woman for his wife. Surely if he offered marriage, she would see he was serious. He was a resolute and prompt man, and it took him only a few weeks to ask her hand for marriage, as though there was no one to be considered in the matter but himself and his own will.

Afsana was silent, her eyes fixed on the ground, her hands lying quietly on her lap. Shiraj stood in silence for a while, desperate to convince her of his genuine intent. Coming quite close to her, he took one of her hands in his own. Then he spoke in a low, intense voice, with gentle persuasion and affection.

"I love you, and I've loved you since we were young. You are the only woman I ever asked to marry me. I will not rest till this hand of yours is pledged to me in marriage." His cheeks flushed and his eyes sparkled with evident happiness.

She did not look up at first, as she was overwhelmed with contending emotions.

"Do you not believe that you can love me?" he asked her.

"I don't know. I am not worthy of your love, and I am not the same as I was. I am very grateful to you, very grateful for all the kindness you've shown me."

"Try to get well," he replied kindly. "You are the same to me, Afsana. I'm really delighted—honestly delighted—to see you again, and to see you getting well. I have often thought about you."

She flushed. "If you truly desire this, I will marry you, Shiraj."

After the initial joy of the moment, Shiraj began to think

how his family would raise their eyes and wag their tongues over this atypical marriage. He and Afsana would be outcasts from their own community. He was also not sure that his father would give his consent to this marriage. Shiraj hoped that his father would relent at some future time. And once his father's anger abated, surely he would slowly relent, and things would be back to normal. They would come to love Afsana and understand. Shiraj failed to foresee the consequences of such a quick decision or to take the matter into fuller consideration before committing himself.

And events soon proved how false such a hope was.

"Have you written to your father about us?" Afsana asked one afternoon as she sat in her room.

"No. I've been thinking about it, but I think it's better to tell him in person, when I go home on leave."

"But if we are to marry soon, he should be let into your decision. Why wait until you get leave? My condition will be obvious soon. Don't you think it would be better if he knows before that?"

Shiraj was quiet for a moment, and then he began very slowly. "I wish I were sure about his reaction. He will be most unhappy if the marriage is not arranged by him. He'll disapprove of any girl his son brings home, even if she is the one they would have chosen for me."

"You don't really mean that he will object simply on that account. Your father is so fond of you, and you were an obedient child all your life. I remember I always thought your father was a kind person."

"Yes, he is, Afsana, but when it comes to marriage, well, it's not quite so simple." But the disappointment on his future wife's face was enough to compel him to action.

~

A rough, stormy wind was blowing when Shiraj knocked at the door of his parents' house. Trees on the drive creaked and groaned beneath the pressure of the gusty winds, but all was warm and snug inside the house. Shiraj's father welcomed him home and invited him to sit. His father stretched out in comfort on the sofa, soon joined by his mother. Shiraj chose his favorite old chair and settled in. For half an hour, the two men sat and talked, till at last Shiraj's father roused himself and got to his feet. A tall, heavy man, with thin, white hair, he looked down with an odd smile at Shiraj, who was still relaxing in the deepest chair.

"Don't go to bed yet, Shiraj," he began. "We have something important to discuss."

When he didn't continue, Shiraj prompted him. "Out with it, Abbu."

"It is time you marry. We have delayed long enough. I have found a girl who will suit you admirably, the youngest daughter of my distant cousin. I hope to start talking about marriage negotiations soon and then we can set the date."

Shiraj felt a sort of panic wash over him at these words. He opened and closed his mouth, angry with himself for not sharing his news first. His mother looked at him with a curious tightening of her features but spoke no word. He struggled to control the swell of emotion that was surging through him as wildly as the storm that beat outside upon the windowpanes.

"I can't—I mean, it is impossible for me to marry your cousin's daughter."

His father frowned. "What do you mean? Why is it impossible?"

"Because I don't love her."

"Shiraj, my son, what one looks for in a wife are a good character and a good background. If you find a woman like that to put her hand in yours, you'll be a lucky man and a happy man."

Shiraj replied, "And if that woman has all those qualities plus you love her, then you will be luckier and happier. Abbu, I came home to discuss an important matter with you and I ask for patience. I have found a girl who has all the good qualities and who has captured my heart as well."

His father started pacing back and forth.

"Whose daughter is she?"

"She is Afsana. You may remember her parents from when I was young. I can assure you that she is a perfectly wonderful person, and I know that I could never find a better wife. She is the only girl I can marry."

"Just like that? You have decided? You will not abide by your parents' wishes?"

Shiraj looked to his mother for support, but she lowered her eyes.

"She is a good person. You will support my decision when you meet her. And she is not a complete stranger. We grew up together."

Shiraj expected a raging storm and fierce resistance, but his father just walked away into his room, closing the door behind him.

When Shiraj arrived at breakfast the next morning, a heavy silence hung over the kitchen.

His father spoke evenly and calmly. "I find your decision deviant, sinful, and particularly disrespectful, Shiraj."

"You will change your mind, Abbu, when you come to know her."

"I will not, because I will never see her and I will have nothing to do with her. Furthermore, I won't have you in my house any longer. You are no longer welcome here."

Shaking, Shiraj gathered his things and departed, sure that his father would eventually relent.

Shiraj invited his parents to the wedding, but his stubborn father dug in and refused to come. In lieu of a wedding gift, his father sent a message that he disowned and disinherited his only son for marrying the girl against his approval.

The letter stunned Afsana, who wept bitterly at the pain and sorrow she caused her new husband. "This is how we begin our life together? Shunned and cast aside? We are alone in the world now. I knew you would regret your decision."

"I regret nothing, Afsana," Shiraj assured her. "My father is a good man, a deeply family-oriented man, and one day he will look more kindly on our marriage."

Despite her disappointment, and the concern she had ruined her husband's life, Afsana began her journey toward motherhood with joy and courage and unwavering support from Shiraj. Throughout her experience of queasy mornings, sleepless nights, countless visits to the bathroom, and the dull throbbing in her back, she was amazed by her body's ability to create a new life, the way her mother and grandmother and all her great-grandmothers had done.

She slowly embraced her pregnancy. She was delighted when the new life stirred inside her, a little flutter of movement deep within. She and Shiraj both teared up when they heard a tiny heartbeat for the first time. Soon, playful kicks and thumps reminded Afsana that she was not alone.

Afsana fell more in love with Shiraj every day, as he asked her how he could help and offered to take on some new responsibilities to lighten her load.

"I do not wish to wait until the child's arrival to connect with our baby," Shiraj told her. "I want this baby born knowing my voice, knowing its father will care for mother and child every day."

Her blouses were getting tighter. She could no longer close the buttons, and she felt her hips had widened too. Shiraj took her shopping for clothing to accommodate her expanding belly, now full and round. She frowned in the mirror at her bloated face. When she suggested to Shiraj that he must find her repulsive, he laughed and assured her she was only more beautiful to him.

All the women she encountered commented on how high she was carrying the child and predicted she would have a daughter. That combined with her strong craving for sweets confirmed it for them. "This is a girl," she was told over and over, by women nodding with their firm belief.

Since there were no internal exams at the moment, Shiraj was included in her office visits, measuring her growing stomach and listening to the fetal heartbeat on a special stethoscope.

"No need to worry," he would chime in, patting her hand. "Everything is looking perfectly normal. You're going to have an easy delivery."

But no amount of assurances made Afsana feel comfortable. She doubted her ability to raise a child and wondered how Shiraj would react when he laid eyes on the child. Despite his determination to be this child's father, what would happen in the moment? Would he regret everything and view another man's child in disgust? Divorce her and accept his father's choice of wife to bring peace to his family? Only time would tell.

After several months, she woke up in the middle of the night having sporadic and weak contractions. She had Shiraj call the hospital to say she was in labor, but he was told to wait till the contractions were coming regularly and getting stronger. He stayed awake with her all night, holding her hand and timing the contractions and the intervals between them. By morning, it was time to go.

In the labor room, the midwife examined her as Shiraj paced the room. The bedside light was on, as well as a spotlight at the foot of the bed. A pediatric nurse and a female technician stood on hand, waiting for the delivery. The midwife sat at the foot of the bed and coached Afsana through the labor. Afsana thought the intense pain would rip her insides apart.

"It's time to push!" the midwife announced finally.

Shiraj sat at the head of the bed, holding her hand and

relaying instructions into her ear. Exhaustion overtook her. Eventually, she lay back, no more to give to this process. Shiraj leaned close, his gaze steady.

"Push, Afsana, my strong girl. You can do this. Push, and push hard, and it will all be over."

She rallied and gave a final push. Relief overcame her. It was over.

The midwife cried, "Put out your hands."

She reached out and accepted the helpless, wailing thing.

"My poor little one. So scared." She held her baby and stroked her tiny body as the midwife cleared her mouth and nose. The nurse took the infant and swaddled her, then gently placed the baby back in Afsana's arms.

"You have a beautiful baby girl!" the nurse said.

"Yes, we do, and she looks just like her mother." Shiraj sighed deeply.

He looked tenderly at her, then at their baby.

Afsana gazed at the bundle that stirred in the hollow of her arms—a tightly fisted baby, who had just entered the world with the lusty wail of a newborn child. She was so full of life. Her heart swelled with a mother's pride and love as she looked at her, then she gave a little sigh, faintly foreshadowing the pain this lovely, willful creature might one day cause her.

Shiraj held the baby's finger for a blissful half hour. He and Afsana looked into each other's eyes, and then he turned suddenly and gathered them both in his arms.

"How much I've wanted you, my sweetheart!"

Shiraj could not refrain from crying tears of joy. He named the newborn baby Razia Sultana, after the last queen of Bengal before British rule.

"Don't you think it's a beautiful name?"

"Yes, it's a beautiful name, my dear, and I love it. Wait until she giggles," she whispered. "And her eyes, they are so brown!"

Even thinking about it brought tears to Afsana's eyes. She loved and appreciated Shiraj's hard work and sacrifices so that she could live the life she wanted. The trust and comfort were so empowering and relieving. It was something, Afsana thought, that solidified the journey toward oneness they had experienced through the whole process of parenthood. Her heart was filled with nothing but gratitude as Shiraj stayed home those first few weeks to help her, taking over all the household chores and delighting in holding the baby.

In her solitude, however, there came a point when she sat back to reflect on her relationship with her first husband, Farzad —what he taught her, what she learned about love. And the nuggets of self-knowledge she gleaned along the way. Now she was acutely aware of her surroundings and her senses, almost as if a dark cloud had been lifted from her soul. And she could live her life to its fullest potential. She remembered Farzad with kind memories, memories that were now of the past. She had loved him, yet what could love have to do with the feeling she was having now? So what if she loved him? He was dead, but she was alive as she'd never been before. She was in the present, and she had her own identity.

Fourteen

THE BOLD AND THE BEAUTIFUL

When Nafisa was released from the army barracks, she wandered anxiously through the abandoned streets of Dhaka, not knowing what to do with her newly acquired freedom. She was confused and disoriented. Fear and isolation engulfed her completely. A passerby discovered her sitting forlornly and took her to a makeshift shelter for women who were abducted during the war. She was then taken to a rehabilitation center for long-term care and counseling for survivors, entrusting medical practitioners with the task of dealing with unwanted pregnancies and adoption campaigns for babies that had been abandoned. After a long wait, the doctor confirmed her pregnancy. He discussed options with her, giving her hope and assurance. "The government has waived the abortion law in . . . situations like yours. Women who were . . . mistreated by Pakistani soldiers during the war may end their pregnancies."

"Could you please contact my family? They may know what I am supposed to do, whether I should have the baby or not." Surely her parents would help her to raise their grandchild.

Nafisa's parents came to see her and comforted her as best as they could.

"Can I come home with you now?" she asked them.

For a moment, her father made no reply. Tears leaked from behind his glasses and rolled in torrents down his cheeks. "Not now, Nafisa. Our home was partially destroyed by the military invasions, and we are in the process of repairing it. It is not the right time to take you home. They'll take good care of you here."

Nafisa turned toward her mother for some assurance but was disappointed to see her reaction. Her mother would barely look at her. Nafisa knew that her condition could be enough to tarnish her family's reputation. The disgrace of a family member was inevitably a humiliation to others in the family. Her brother Nasir was still unmarried. She suspected her mother feared that her son would not be able to marry a girl from a reputable family. Still, Nafisa held out hope her parents would not abandon her. Where would she go if they did not accept her? Who would take care of her?

"We'll come back for you, Nafisa, once the house is fixed." Her mother attempted to smile, but Nafisa saw the truth in her eyes.

The pity of her family wrapped her up in a cruel, whispering sympathy, shut her lips, sealed her eyes as hopelessness and desperation grew within her.

Left on her own, Nafisa decided to have the baby. Perhaps it would be more correct to say that, unable to make a decision, she carried on as best she could and her stomach swelled, the new life continuing to grow and develop whether Nafisa wanted it or not.

And when the day came for it to be born, and labor pains wracked her body, the baby of an unknown father, conceived under brutal circumstances, was ushered into the world unceremoniously, outside of wedlock.

She cursed God, whom she had hitherto considered kind, fair, and just. As the screams of pain forced their way through her clenched teeth, her inner being rose up in an angry revolt, furious with hatred for the man who had ruined her life and an intense disgust for this unknown child.

Finally, a seemingly endless number of excruciating hours later, she pushed hard. Immense relief followed. As she lay there, breathing heavily, recovering from the ordeal, a little bundle was placed in her arms. She looked at the stirring bit of life in her arms—and finally made a choice. She would give him up for adoption.

Nafisa spent the rest of her day in the dreary solitude of her room and then relieved her heart with another burst of tears. She wept for hours, went to bed, and cried herself to sleep. She, who had always been so strong and sure, could not decide what was the right choice.

When morning came, the bright sun cast the problem in a new light. Nafisa had no more tears to shed. She walked toward the nursery where her son was bundled up in a cot. She picked him up, held him close, and whispered into his ear.

"I have no other choice but to give you up. I'm sure someday, someone with a kind heart will raise you as their own. You'll have a far better life than if you stay with me when I have nothing to offer you."

Nafisa left the rehab center. Weak and faint, abandoned by family, longing for some place where she might rest, she had no place to go. With a drooping heart and weary limbs, she joined the river of humanity trudging along toward the Indian border to an unknown future. On the other side of the border, she would become a refugee—a stranger in a strange land. The line of barely clothed refugees with empty stomachs was so long that Nafisa was not able to see the other end. Some of them were walking, some limping, old and crippled, being carried in baskets by able-bodied men in bamboo yokes, balancing them on their strong muscled shoulders. Everyone moved in one direction. She saw strange faces on every side, strange voices filling the air.

They traveled longer distances in bullock-cart convoys to reach a ferry point, from where they continued by an overloaded truck, bus, or larger river craft. Traveling twenty to thirty miles would take eight to ten hours. Day by day they trekked. At night, they turned off their clay lamps and lanterns for fear of detection by the army.

She, like many others, took one of the primitive modes of transportation for longer distances, a crowded bullock-cart, to reach the rail station. Nafisa sat in silence during these endless, plodding trips and stared at the sweaty flanks of the bulls, their tails endlessly twitching, brushing away flies, which settled on her face instead.

Once she reached the train station, she boarded an equally crowded train that took her to a refugee camp site. She was shown to a dreary and uncomfortable lean-to. The camp had clearly been thrown together to attempt to handle the onslaught of refugees.

The days were nothing but hours of grueling and repetitive daily chores, such as collecting clean water to drink and to use for washing, cooking, and cleaning. Queuing for relief rations in the camp was an added task for her. Reduced food rations sometimes reduced her and the other homeless refugees to near starvation. Though they were given excuses, she heard rumors that the camp officials stole the food. Sometimes fights broke out as refugees accused others of making false claims for more than their share of rations.

How she missed Dhaka with the stretches of open spaces, clusters of inviting houses, and neatly spaced mango trees, banana trees, and coconut trees. And the serene bamboo groves. She longed for home.

Instead, she found herself in the cramped living quarters of the camp, one of untold millions of displaced people. She could see India was attempting to accommodate, but the sheer number of people was impossible to handle.

As she sat silently dreaming of home, her neighbors were putting a child to sleep. Others were separating the rationed rice from stone chips. A small cooking fire warmed a pot. A few feet away from her tiny tent, a little boy sat crumpled and crying, flies gathering on his emaciated body. Nafisa thought of her own abandoned little boy and was glad he wasn't here, subject to the harsh conditions. She prayed he was somewhere safe and warm, being fed and loved.

As the days went by, Nafisa wearied of fending off advances of officials, who abducted and trafficked women and girls on a regular basis. She closed her eyes against the sight of women dragged from their tents but could not block out the pleas for help. Other women gave up and engaged in the world's oldest profession willingly, knowing they would receive better and more rations for their efforts. The refugee camp was not the respite she had hoped for when she fled home. Here, Nafisa faced a new type of horror.

As the weeks went on, malnutrition and epidemics of cholera and dysentery plagued the refugees. Minimal medical services led to outbreaks of all kinds of diseases. The refugees died faster than they could be buried. She had to pass by the dead bodies of cholera victims that were left on the sides of roads by their friends and relatives, as they were too frightened of catching the disease themselves to take the time to bury them. Hordes of vultures fought over the corpses—a feeling of revulsion rose in her and her sordid surroundings.

She knew she must leave this place and try her luck elsewhere. After six months in the refugee camp, Nafisa began to explore the streets of noisy Calcutta in order to get better acquainted with the way of life in the city, in hopes she could find a way to make a home there. She would never return to Dhaka. Her family had forgotten her, she was sure. She would make a new life somehow here in India. Amidst the clamor and confusion of the big city, she wandered alone, friendless, unsupported. But being alone was vastly preferable to the decay and disease of camp.

And, as fate would have it, she crossed paths with someone quite unexpectedly.

~

"Good heavens!" Afsana gasped when she ran into her friend in a busy market. "Nafisa! Is that you?"

"Afsana! Am I awake? Is this real? I dreamed that I'd find you someday but never believed it would really happen."

The two women walked together through the clamor of the streets, sharing the horrors they had experienced since they'd been separated in Dhaka.

Afsana stopped, no idea how much time had passed as they wandered aimlessly. "I am so sorry for what you've been through, but so happy to see you."

"Likewise. I wish I had found you sooner."

"Nasir didn't find you, then?"

"I have not seen Nasir or heard from him. I thought . . . I worried he—"

"Your brother is safe and alive," Afsana assured her friend. "He went to the army camps looking for you but found me instead. I escaped with his help."

Nafisa brightened. "If Nasir is alive, perhaps Saif also survived the war. Perhaps there is still hope for the future! If I can find him, if he can overlook the—"

"Nafisa, Nasir and I encountered Saif during our escape. I am so sorry. He didn't make it."

"Then I have truly lost it all." And she broke down in sobs.

"There is always hope," Afsana attempted to console her friend.

"No. I left out the worst part of my story. Perhaps I ought to have told you earlier, but the shame of it was so acute that I couldn't talk about it."

Afsana rested a hand on Nafisa's shoulder. Her stomach turned as she suspected she already knew about this shame.

"I . . . had a baby. One of the soldiers in the barracks . . ."

Afsana threw her arms around Nafisa and hugged her close. "It's okay. It's not your fault. Where is your little one?"

Nafisa sobbed harder. "I gave him up for adoption. What else could I have done other than what I did? But now I shall never see my baby again!"

"Did your parents never know about the baby?" Afsana asked her.

"They knew. They came to see me in the rehabilitation center. But they wouldn't take me home. They left me there to deal with it alone."

Afsana rubbed her friend's back. How would she have handled her own situation, had Shiraj not found and helped her? "I'm so sorry."

"I held him in my arms, a beautiful, healthy baby boy. And then I left him."

"We will find him someday," Afsana said, though she doubted the words as she spoke them. Nothing else would console her grieving friend. "He is surely thriving and taken care of. I know he has made some woman very happy."

"And you have a daughter," Nafisa said. "Does she favor your new husband?"

Afsana hesitated. "Everyone says she looks exactly like me."

Nafisa lifted her head and dried her tears. "Then she is beautiful. What a blessing. I would love to see her."

"You shall. You're coming with me. Let's go."

Fifteen

AN UNREQUITED LOVE

As the two women approached Afsana's home, Nafisa held back as if nervous.

"Shiraj is very kind," Afsana said. "You have nothing to fear."

Nafisa's wide eyes traveled over the home Afsana and Shiraj had made their own. After Shiraj's father disowned him, Shiraj had purchased the house here in Calcutta. "It's . . . so nice, Afsana. I don't know if I can do this."

Afsana took her friend's hand and pulled her close, then opened the door.

"Shiraj! I have wonderful news! Guess who I met today in the market. My oldest and best friend, Nafisa!"

Shiraj stepped out of his office. His gaze landed on the two women and a huge smile spread over his face. "This is Nafisa? However did you happen to find one another?"

"We were both in the market. I looked up, and there she was."

"This explains your lengthy absence. In the best possible way. Come in! Let us make some tea for you."

Afsana settled Nafisa into a chair and joined Shiraj in the

kitchen. They spoke in hushed tones so that Nafisa could not hear them.

"She looks terrible," Shiraj murmured. "What in God's name has happened to her?"

"The same thing that happened to me, except she was not fortunate enough to have someone rescue her as you rescued me." Afsana, overcome with another wave of gratefulness, hugged her husband.

"She is emaciated," Shiraj said, his doctor's brain assessing this new "patient" who had come through his door. "She is clearly starving. I think we should feed her a good meal at least before she goes."

Afsana hesitated, choosing her words carefully. "I knew you would want to help her. I think it is necessary for her to stay with us for a time."

Shiraj stopped rustling through the pantry, gathering food for their guest. "Has she no family?"

"She says they rejected her, Shiraj." She let that hang in the air, as they both knew what rejection felt like. "She has no one."

"And yet she, like so many others, is rejected not for her actions but from horrors committed against her. The Bangladeshi government is calling them *birangona*, war heroines, and has forbidden anyone from condemning them."

"Nafisa's parents must not have heard this. Or perhaps they do not care." Afsana realized the term *birangona* applied to herself but did not share this with her husband. She did not feel like a war heroine and doubted any of the others in her situation did either. *And no one knows what to do with us.*

"I've read articles . . . hundreds of thousands of women were raped in this war. The Pakistanis abducted and are still holding hundreds of women. The new Bangladeshi government is attempting to free them, but some of the women barely speak after liberation." He shuddered and pulled Afsana to him. "I cannot bear the thought of you mistreated in this way. It is too horrible. These women should be supported and helped, not ostracized and condemned."

"Then, she can stay with us? This is our chance to help."

"We do owe your life to her brother, Nasir. If he hadn't rescued you, we never would have been reunited."

"And I would be in her predicament."

The two stared at one another, clearly both imagining this alternate version of history, where Nasir did not find Afsana and she languished in prison and refugee camps, ending up like Nafisa—and so many other women Shiraj saw and treated each day.

"It is settled," Shiraj said, a grim determination on his face. "She will move in with us until she is able to establish a new life here in Calcutta."

Afsana squeezed her sweet and generous husband in a hug. "Thank you, Shiraj."

Nafisa broke down in tears when Afsana told her the news. "I could not . . . this is too much. Are you certain?"

"We have decided," Afsana assured her. "I will show you to your room and then we can go get your things from where you have been living."

Afsana led her to the spare room. On the way, they passed Razia's nursery. Nafisa peered inside, at the baby in the crib. She broke away from Afsana and approached the infant as if entranced. She sank to her knees beside the bed where the child was sleeping. She made no sound and shed no tears—perhaps the anguish that racked her was too deep to make such expressions. With her hungry eyes, she devoured the sleeper.

"Oh, Nafisa." Afsana knelt beside her friend. "I cannot imagine what you are feeling. Will you be okay here?"

Nafisa gripped a fistful of the blanket but didn't respond.

"Give her a place in your heart. Razia is God sent. She is a blessing to us both. One day she'll prove herself to be her name-sake—an angel in our home to light up the darkness that has overshadowed it for so long."

At that moment, as if realizing something profound happened and centered around her, Razia opened her eyes and stared directly at Nafisa. A tiny smile lifted the corners of her mouth.

Tears broke through Nafisa's stony countenance. "My child! I'll take her in my arms. She will be my baby, too."

Afsana relaxed in relief. She lifted the child and nestled the bundle into Nafisa's arms. "And from now on, Razia will have two mothers. You will love her as your own. I am sure your help in raising, nurturing, and loving her will give you immense joy and happiness."

Nafisa pulled the baby into a tight embrace, holding her close as if the pressure of the little girl on her chest could lessen the pain in her heart. She wrapped the soft blanket around herself and Razia to keep her warm and secure.

Nafisa moved in. Afsana and Shiraj helped her collect her meager belongings from the refugee camp, leaving the dismal place behind. Smiles and laughter dominated as they situated her in their home. Afsana took Nafisa to market and purchased new clothing and necessary items.

Having her friend nearby brought a piece of home to Afsana. The women shared the household tasks, cooked and ate together, and slowly shared horrific tidbits of information about fleeing from the war. The independence Afsana and Farzad—and Nasir and Saif—had fought for resulted in the nation of Bangladesh, but they could not now enjoy it. Their days at Dhaka University, sitting under the beautiful banyan tree, seemed so long ago. Another life.

Sharing Razia proved a very happy situation, a task both Afsana and Nafisa enjoyed. Quite often, they idled away lazy afternoons in between their chores talking quietly about things in general, the happy infant between them. Life went on in the same manner—peaceful, serene, and uneventful. With the household tasks divided by two, Afsana had more free time and was no longer as overwhelmed with motherhood.

Months passed happily, the horrors of war receded—or at least were pushed aside as much as possible. When Razia took her first steps, they were from Afsana to Nafisa, a delighted smile on her face as she toddled between her two mothers. But then Nafisa scooped the girl into her arms and cried, "Well done! That's my smart girl!"

Something ugly stirred in Afsana's heart. She began watching Nafisa more closely and noticed that as the days rolled on, she became overbearing and overprotective in her dealings with Razia. While trying to form a strong emotional bond with her child as her real mother, Afsana felt threatened by the shadow mother, who failed to recognize her "place" to be simultaneously present and absent in Razia's life. The intricacies of a relationship between two women who shared the responsibility of raising a child began to unfold.

One beautiful afternoon, Nafisa remarked, "I think Razia needs to take a nap. I can put her in bed while you finish up with the cooking."

The words were simple enough but delivered in a commanding tone. Afsana felt as though Nafisa was trying to assert herself on her, giving orders and expecting Afsana to follow her commands. Nafisa seemed overly concerned whenever Razia was upset, catering to her every whim. And she began to worry too much over trivial matters.

Meanwhile, Afsana could not ignore Razia smiling and clinging to Nafisa instead of her. She would reach for Nafisa instead of her own mother whenever she became upset. Afsana wanted to be the one her daughter would turn to when seeking comfort. She began to fear Nafisa's over-attachment, her overprotective solicitousness. While Razia had awakened Nafisa's maternal instincts, pushed aside when she gave her own baby up for adoption, Afsana's motherly instincts put her on guard.

Afsana also detected some changes in Nafisa. She surmised the disappointments in life were to blame for the sudden angry outbursts that seemed to come from nowhere. Afsana felt as though Nafisa wished to take away everything that belonged to her. Her friend not only inserted herself more and more with Razia, but also with the household chores, meals, and decisions that were not hers to make. Afsana could not bring herself to admonish Nafisa directly. Instead, she slowly took upon herself all the tasks of nurturing her own child and running her own household, stepping in before Nafisa could handle things.

A fierce competition began to develop.

~

Nafisa felt the deprivation of all the privileges of being a secondary mother deeply. As she began to see less of Razia, the closeness that she used to enjoy was taken away. Combined with the loss of household chores, her days were left empty. Nafisa needed something to occupy her time.

She longed for someone to love her, but Razia's love was being denied. Jealousy took hold. She wanted a husband to take care of her, as Afsana had Shiraj to care for her. She watched the intimate moments between the two—the glances, the soft caresses, the understanding in quiet moments.

Nafisa began to experience different emotions, which she had never felt before. After her brutal treatment in the prison camp, she had feared and avoided men. Shiraj's gentle nature and easy company soothed her. She thrilled to the touch of his hand when she passed Razia to him. Her pulse quickened and her heart throbbed when he entered the room or they walked by each other in hallways. She began to imagine the type of intimate moments she observed between husband and wife, but with her in Afsana's place.

She noted every glance, every look, every expression. The kind words he had said to her. She was afraid of and uncertain about the feelings that he could stir in her with only a look or a touch of his fingers. What was it about him that caused such battling emotions to the point of falling in love with him so desperately?

Nafisa studied the lovely face of Afsana and became aware of having a formidable rival in her. How had she never before noticed how beautiful Afsana was? No wonder Shiraj had fallen under her spell. If events had unfolded differently, she might have been by his side. Resentment began to build. Nasir should have rescued his sister instead of Afsana. Then perhaps she could have met Shiraj first and would be enjoying this beautiful home and raising her baby boy with this kind-hearted and loving man.

At times, she could not resist indulging her desire. He was so attractive. She began to seek his attention by asking some trivial question or making a remark. Anything to invite him into conversation. The subtle signals of interest in every word that he uttered were surely not all in her imagination. All her efforts filled her with both hope and despair, tormenting her silently.

Nafisa began to bring Shiraj his cup of tea in the evening when he came back from work. This daily, conventional task was normally fulfilled by Afsana with much love and care. Nafisa had to time things carefully in order to beat Afsana to the kitchen and prepare the tea to his liking. Seeing his face light up made up for the consternation Afsana expressed when she realized Nafisa had taken this moment away again.

She waited eagerly to be with Shiraj in her spare hours and especially looked forward to dinnertime. She chose to sit next to him, to be near him, even though there were other empty seats. Her heart would be filled with sadness when he seated himself next to his wife. Those were the days when she felt completely left out, degraded, as if she were made small, unworthy of sitting next to him. But her heart leaped in great joy when he fussed about her lack of appetite in low tones and passed a bowl of rice or fish curry toward her. He clearly cared about her. She would renew her efforts with great enthusiasm after these brief but encouraging moments.

But to her great dismay, she did not make any progress—nothing indicated any change from brotherly friendship to love.

Still, she hoped against hope. Notwithstanding the struggle and conflict and pain, something constantly beat and throbbed —an irresistible hope—that in time he would love her. If only he had been hers. Since Afsana found him first, she would work harder to win his affections to herself.

The dream had formed when she had been dazzled by his dark eyes. When she thought about it, it did not seem like a wise dream as it sprang from an impossibility, an absolute impossibility, forever unattainable. She also realized that should she succeed in winning Shiraj, it would be the ultimate betrayal to her friend, the one person in the world who had acted to help her. There was something sinister, ominously threatening about it all, and she knew she had no right to raise her hopes. She tried not to think too hard about it.

Whatever hopes had been kindled by his looks, by the affection in his voice, or the warmth in his kind eyes, he did nothing to encourage her, nothing that hinted at the smallest possibility of a future together. He kept the relationship platonic and never once crossed the line. The agony it produced in her went far beyond mere jealousy. She questioned her own worth and at times asked herself whether her life did not rest upon a gigantic lie.

Shiraj, amicable to his core, kept a pleasant word for everyone. The admiration of Nafisa amused him and gratified his vanity but certainly never touched his heart. He regarded her shy advances as being nothing but friendly gestures, a way of showering gratitude toward him.

Then gradually, these small attentions from Nafisa, her slavish devotion, and her enthusiasm to please him, took a definite shape. Shiraj became aware that they all pointed to one thing—Nafisa seemed to harbor strong feelings for him.

He reproached himself for such a thought, attempting to write it off as his imagination, yet he could not drive it completely away.

The suspicion haunted him, made him miserable. If it were so, if Nafisa had developed inappropriate feelings for him, what was he to do? His face flushed hotly at the thought.

He began to notice how pale she looked in his presence and realized why she picked at her food at mealtimes, merely moving it around her plate, untouched. He watched how she brought him tea when he returned from work, something Afsana had always tended to, and how solicitous she was as she approached him with a gentle smile and welcomed him home.

Once he noticed these changes, he saw them constantly. How timid and awkward Nafisa was when she talked to him, trying hard to conceal her feelings for him, at the same time obviously craving his love. She revealed the secret of her heart unconsciously and unsuspectingly long before she herself knew there was a secret to reveal.

As Shiraj watched her, he could not help but see her flinging charm around her so that he was insensibly attracted by it. Her voice seemed to take another tone addressing him, and her face had another expression. He could not think that her infatuation had taken deep root in her heart. He cared a great deal for her and considered her as he would a sister.

He did not love her—he was not the least in love. It was only admiration, liking, but not love—anything but that. And what sort of a love was it that was on one side only? He was almost certain that neither by word, sign, nor action had he hinted at any return of her feelings.

Shiraj continued to be as attentive and kind to her as usual but was more careful and reserved in his manner than before. He did not engage in unnecessary conversation or attempt to prolong interactions between them. Eventually, he could see in her face that she suspected the truth—he was aware of her infatuation. Then came the misery of shame and the accompanying awkwardness. Where once Nafisa was shy and endearing in his presence, now she was uncomfortable. The anxiety in the room affected them all. They became uneasy in each other's presence and yet neither could speak about the developing situation for fear of the consequences of voicing their concerns. Left unsaid, the confusing emotions festered. When she came into the room, he would hurry out as fast as he could. He did not want to be the cause of Nafisa being turned out onto the street but had no idea how to repair the broken relationship without jeopardizing her friendship with Afsana. Or worse, raising suspicion in his wife when he had done nothing untoward.

On the other hand, very little ever escaped Afsana's keen eyes. Her womanly instincts did not fail to notice. She began to perceive Nafisa as being something of a threat to her happy home. She saw the way Nafisa behaved around Shiraj. The discomfort that developed between the two assured her the affections were rebuffed—until an ugly voice in her head whispered that perhaps it was the result of something happening between the two.

Whatever had or hadn't happened—and Afsana could not bring herself to ask, for fear of what she might discover—Nafisa was a disruption to her relationship with Shiraj. She knew she had to intervene or run the risk of wrecking her marriage. She would either snip a budding affair or uproot the plant before it could bloom at all.

Afsana reclined upon the sofa and tried to compose herself sufficiently to think of what she was going to say to her friend without hurting her feelings. She called to Nafisa to join her. Her friend entered, looking awkward and uncomfortable, as if caught misbehaving. But then, lately, that was how she always appeared.

"Nafisa, I don't want anything to end our friendship," she told her. "But I have some concerns."

Nafisa shifted uncomfortably. "I don't know what concerns you could have. I've done nothing to hurt you."

Afsana decided now was not the time to be delicate. "You love Shiraj, don't you?"

Nafisa turned deadly pale. "Love him! What makes you think that? Are you so insecure in your relationship? He obviously doesn't care for anyone but you."

Afsana did not miss the note of jealousy in that last statement. She narrowed her eyes. "I do know that you are playing with his feelings. I see the way you behave around him."

"I am not being flirtatious. All I do is to make myself a little agreeable."

"Are you not aware that he is falling in love with you?" Afsana's heart broke as she spoke the words, fearing truth in them.

Nafisa leaned away, as if truly taken aback. And yet, she seemed somehow pleased by this. "He has feelings for me?"

"So you admit your love for him?"

"It isn't fair! You have hope. You have a beautiful husband and daughter and home. The world is at your feet! But I have lost everything. How do I begin again?"

"Not by stealing my husband," Afsana said.

Nafisa spoke in a torrent of unleashed words, as if they'd been building for some time and longing for escape. "I never meant to fall in love with him. It crept up on me slowly, little by little. I don't know how it all began. He's just so kind and attentive. And you must be aware how attractive he is."

"He is a married man, Nafisa. My husband."

"I try to avoid him. But that is difficult when we all live here together." Genuine anguish seemed to creep into her voice. "If you are my true friend, you will not blame me, Afsana."

"Your true friend? I brought you into my home. And this is how you thank me? Your own parents did nothing to help you! I did!" Shame immediately filled Afsana's heart. "I'm sorry. That was wrong."

"No, you are right," Nafisa whispered, her cheeks burning pink. "I have done wrong to you. You showed me kindness when I was at my lowest and when no one else did. I ask you to forgive me."

Afsana saw through the brave front Nafisa tried to put forth, heard her voice quaver as she wiped her eyes. "I forgive you. But how do we move forward now?"

Nafisa nodded. "I will go."

Afsana suspected Nafisa hoped they would insist she stay. But she could not find it in her heart to encourage this to continue. "I think perhaps that is for the best."

Shiraj had learned of a program to train the *birangona* in Bangladesh—women were trained for secretarial work or sewing and crafts so that they could potentially earn money and support themselves. In reality, however, society was not prepared for a huge influx of women into the workforce. Of the ten million who had fled Bangladesh, many were attempting to return home, only to find entire towns in ruin.

Nafisa did not wish to return to Bangladesh, and Afsana could not blame her. The desire to go home could never be satisfied when home no longer existed. The women longed for a return to a simpler time, an innocence, that could never be rebuilt. The best they could do was gather their tattered lives about them and stitch it back together into a semblance of normal.

Nafisa had everything packed up within a few days. As her departure rapidly approached, Afsana and Shiraj had an argument about her leaving their house.

"If she refuses to return and join the training program, where will she go? It isn't right to throw her out!" Shiraj remarked.

"That isn't our problem anymore." Afsana was furious to hear her husband defending another woman—a woman who threatened their marriage. "It's much better that she go. We found a solution. We cannot make her accept it. I am sure she will find something."

"How can you claim to be her friend and treat her so callously?"

"I will not listen to you turn her into a victim. She has been throwing herself at you in my own home, before my eyes!"

"Afsana, what on earth are you implying?"

"Oh, I see her. I watch her. I am not blind. And I know what it means when a woman looks at a man that way."

"Whatever do you mean?"

"Don't play dumb," she chastised him. "She admitted her feelings for you to me."

Shiraj waved a hand as though dismissing Afsana's concerns. "Feelings. What? A small crush? It is harmless."

"Harmless? The atmosphere of this house has been so uncomfortably awkward of late that I can barely breathe. That doesn't sound like a harmless crush!"

"You are making something of nothing."

His lackadaisical attitude infuriated her. "And perhaps," she said with a gasp, "the feelings are mutual. I wanted to believe nothing had happened between you, but now I'm not sure what to think!"

"Afsana, be reasonable—"

"Who knows what might have happened if she had stayed. I ought to have known when I saw her envious disposition. First, she tried to steal my child, then my husband!"

The suddenness of the attack appeared to completely dumbfound Shiraj. "I cannot talk with you when you are like this."

He left the room, leaving Afsana more convinced than ever that she had made the correct decision. Her marriage must be saved, even at the expense of her friendship.

Sixteen

A NEW LIFE

Nafisa waited for Shiraj to walk her outside and secretly stood in dread of his first words. She would be quite satisfied if Shiraj would only speak. If he would only say a few words that would set her mind at ease, she would be content. How blind she had been not to see where she was drifting, but there was in her heart a woman's instinct to fight against it. She must give up Shiraj, or rather give up the attempt to win him. She would risk everything if she stayed here any longer.

They were alone in the room for a brief interval. And this was the very room into which she had first been ushered, a friend, welcomed, before she became an inmate, then a burden. Everything seemed unreal to her. How could she leave?

Shiraj entered the room. Her heart began to beat faster as she gave one eager, quick, searching look.

She could not refrain from seizing Shiraj's hand. He looked at her, his own face full of pain, yet he was honor bound to be silent. Though she was going away, he could not speak a word of what had passed between them out of respect for Afsana. He did not shrink from her gaze, though. He stared at her for a moment and then smiled gently. There was some sort of assurance in that look and smile.

Had it been in his power to set the whole matter right with a word, he would probably have spoken the word, but as it was not possible, he must follow up the matter as a man would do in his position.

"Nafisa," he said at length, in a hoarse and husky voice, "you made the right decision to move out. But you'll be visiting us every now and then. And we will come and visit you. You can come and stay with us anytime just like before."

Nafisa felt intense relief when he spoke in his usual manner.

Shiraj hastened to take her hands in his own.

"It's not your fault at all, Nafisa," he said with soft tenderness in his voice. "These happenings are sometimes beyond our control. We are still friends."

She looked away wistfully, aching at the thought he could have been hers, thinking about her own child whom she had to abandon. Life was nothing but a magnificent tapestry woven with threads. And a weaving Creator wove its designs with his wonderful hands. While spinning the thread of her destiny, those very tender hands had woven in a stray strand carelessly and recklessly, deviating from its normal path. So, the fabric of her destiny failed to create a beautiful tapestry. It did not dazzle with brilliance like the others. It had unraveled and was left a jumbled mess. But she was determined to repair it. She would find a way to weave her own happy ending.

She believed that great things came only occasionally, only for the lucky ones, and that sadly in some people's lives they never come. And it was more maddening because, with all the wanting of her heart, she knew such things were simply and purely unattainable. For her.

She was a woman carrying a dark secret, someone who saw the war every day in her mind, felt it in her body, through the birth of her child. Sometimes the agony became so acute that her mind went blank. She failed to radiate happiness when she herself was not happy or to smile when she wanted to cry. She fell into silence when she felt like screaming her anguish. She could not comfort when she needed to be comforted. Yet she lived, like many unfortunate others to whom death would have been an only consolation and an escape from all the miseries of being alive. A lone woman, crying over her lost child—but then it came as a gleam of light to her when she realized that it was God's purpose to keep her alive. He had something better waiting for her. Or perhaps that was what she needed to believe in that moment.

Shiraj gently ushered her into the waiting car. There was a sweetness to the sound of his voice that could only come from him. It dulled the pain of her reluctant departure.

Nafisa heard the gate-latch click behind her. She turned and looked back at the house briefly with lingering and wistful eyes. She had been with them for so many months, yet it scarcely seemed a day.

"How am I to bear it? What am I to do?" she said to herself.

She looked around in bewilderment, with the dazed appearance of one from beneath whose feet a solid plank of safety had been whisked away suddenly. Although she was brave and knew no fear, for a moment she was terrified, and she found herself hopelessly lost. She did break down when she thought about her future stretching out before her—a future that was devoid of love. It was also a crushing blow to her vanity. She did not know how she was going to bear the defeat. But her inner voice told her that all was not lost even though she feared it, and she threw her shoulders back, her chin up, and readied herself to follow her destiny wherever it took her. Whatever they might do to her, they would not crush her or destroy her.

The spirit of her perseverance and her desire to rise above the difficulties of her life carried her through that difficult time. She accepted the job Shiraj had arranged for her in a medical clinic and moved into the small apartment he had secured for her. Within a few months, she was able to take over the payment of rent.

A much older gentleman in the clinic took an interest in her.

And she was drawn to his affections as a bee to a blooming flower. The attention he lavished on her soothed her wounded vanity, rejected as she was by Shiraj. Although he was not the choice of her heart, she married him and finally had a house of her own. She had believed life was over and nothing waited for her in the future but loneliness. And here she was married, with a home to look after.

The touch of her husband's hand holding hers opened the gates of everlasting happiness and a blissful life stretched before her. The first few months of her married life were such bright ones for Nafisa, even though her husband did not bless her with a child, as she hoped he would. She had to give up on that hope. Her dreams of youth remained insubstantial, like gossamer threads floating in the air. Never would she have a home full of children. She thought often about the baby boy she had turned her back on. She put on strong armor, burying the pain of the past so that the memories would stop hurting her.

But her husband had a terrible fondness for alcohol, a secret he kept until late in their first year of marriage. And when he drank in excess, he became angry, sometimes violent.

With the passing of time, she realized that being a wife was nothing but a life of slavery and degradation. He expected her to stay at home, have no friends, cook and clean. The man she was married to turned into a complete stranger and cost her so many tears. Cold, distant, and hostile, there was not a single grain of love in him. He complained bitterly about everything she did or didn't do—dinner was not to his liking, the bed sheets weren't stretched taut enough, the tea was too hot or not hot enough. He took a job that led him frequently away from home. During his absences he often left his wife with no means to support herself. She felt like a fool, duped into marriage to an angry old man who simply wanted a maid and a cook.

Of late, he had been drinking heavily, often not coming in until morning. There were long absences he never explained, he became more and more parsimonious in his dealing with money, denying her everything but the basic necessities of life. Then came the inevitable moment, the final outrage of his drunken raving.

"You've been sitting up again?" He slurred his words.

"I thought you might need some help getting up the stairs," Nafisa said.

"Don't trouble yourself about that. I've come to fetch something and I'll be gone again."

"You're not going out again? I'm tired of being alone. I'll come with you."

"You'll what?"

"Come with you. Being married and alone is worse than having no husband at all."

"You don't mean this."

"Yes, I mean this," she answered. "I cannot bear it."

His face grew darker in the shadows of the room, and she became conscious of those bloodshot eyes looking into her very soul. The perspiration broke out in thick beads on his forehead as he approached her, fists clenched and fury on his face. Shortness of breath almost choked him. His unsteady limbs and ineffectual lurch gave her the fraction of time to escape from his blows. She took refuge in their bedroom and locked the door. After a while, Nafisa heard a heavy fall from behind the closed doors.

When she woke up in the morning he was gone. He left no note, no indication he had even been home the night before. Months dragged heavily into years.

He never came back.

Seventeen

OUT OF WAR, A NEW NATION

The war ended on December 16th, 1971. Nasir, back in Dhaka and still trying to locate his sister, heard that Pakistani forces had held women at Dhaka cantonment. The government was working to liberate these women. On December 20th, Maleka Khan led a group of women armed with rifles into the cantonment to rescue the trapped women. Over several days, they made repeated trips in and brought more women out. But Nafisa was not among them.

One night, he discovered his parents had seen her while she was pregnant. Disappointed with his parents' decision to abandon her when she needed them most, he took it upon himself to rectify the situation and bring both Nafisa and the child home to family.

He interviewed many people, hoping for information about Nafisa and her baby, eventually learning she had given birth to a boy. He visited orphanages, made inquiries, and searched for his nephew for more than a year. Most people either could not or would not assist him. But Nasir would not give up hope of finding them both.

"We wanted to ensure you could marry," his mother told him

frequently. "We had to make the best decision for the family. Give this up and find a nice young woman to take as your bride."

Nasir gritted his teeth, struggling to show proper respect to his parents. "I will not give this up. My sister and her son are out there somewhere. I cannot rest until I know they are safe."

Finally one day, he encountered a woman who took care of his sister at the rehabilitation center. He learned that Nafisa named her child Ayaan and that he had been given up for adoption. But they had no records to indicate which orphanage he had been sent to.

So he simply continued looking. He visited orphanages, made inquiries, and searched for his nephew for more than a year. Most people either could not or would not assist him. But Nasir would not give up hope of finding them both.

In one such visit, in an old, obscure building with no sign or indication that the old house was an orphanage, he discovered small children of different age groups lurking about in the enclosed area of the building. They gazed at him with vacant eyes. He was a total stranger to them, yet they befriended him without any hesitation and called him Abba. They were hungry for affection, craving his love and acceptance. The moment he sat down, several of the younger ones tried to snuggle into his lap. He was shocked and full of dismay at the unspeakable conditions of the children, unkempt and skeletal in appearance. Most of the children were in poor health and some appeared to have chronic diseases.

A worker took Nasir into the interior room where babies spent most of their day—a bare, drab room, not a toy in sight. Sheets hung over the sides of the cribs, obstructing their views.

The toddlers all came to him grinning, jumping, and he was soon surrounded by these barefoot children grasping for his hand. Nasir noticed that they were emotionally drained. One little girl's arm hung at an odd angle. The worker explained she had broken it but received no treatment because of lack of funds. He lifted her up and held her in his arms. The little girl kept staring at him for a long time. He did not find his nephew there. The memory of the children haunted him.

Nasir's relentless search led him to another orphanage, in a remote corner of a quiet street. He stood looking at the rundown building with a courtyard that he never knew existed. It had fallen into a state of disrepair. Presumably, no one had lived there for years.

It was a huge, old house surrounded by a few acres of land. The crumbling walls were covered with creeping vines, and the trees spread their branches over its roof, protecting it from many a rough blast of winter winds. The patched roof was green here and there with moss and blackened with age. And beneath projecting tiles, jutting from the roof, you could hear the flap of pigeon's wings every now and then. The wear and tear told of years of life within it, of times long since passed.

When Nasir approached the rusted wrought-iron gate, he could hear the echoes of the babble of excited children. The orphanage was for boys only, of different age groups. Gaunt walls and bare floors and the absence of a welcoming atmosphere stood out vividly the moment he walked into the building. The younger boys were extremely boisterous and more chaotic than the older boys. They remained confined in gloomy, overcrowded rooms.

To his dismay, a musty odor hung in the air, as if these children had never been thoroughly scrubbed and brushed all their lives. It fairly took away his breath when he leaned to talk to them or hold them. With sparse furnishings, the children sat on the floor. But Nasir was relieved to see that they were learning to recite religious texts. They also learned simple math and their main vernacular. The older boys learned carpentry, shoemaking, and other vocational skills.

In addition to the ramshackle building and its classrooms, there was a narrow room, which served as an eating place, where fifty boys gathered at one table and shared food. Nasir was further dismayed to see how little food sat on the table, and that the food lacked nutritional content.

Searching for a face that had some sort of resemblance to his sister was not an easy task for Nasir. He knew roughly the age his nephew should be, but many of the orphans were especially small for their age, growth stunted by poor nutrition and medical care.

This particular orphanage haunted him. He went back to the place and insisted on seeing the children once again.

He took toys with him, unable to bear the oppressive atmosphere. The boys flocked around him in a tight circle. They had never seen toys before, the worker told him. Their eyes lit up as they shyly reached for the wondrous gifts he'd brought.

One toddler captured his interest. He was different from the others, least affected by what was going on. He stood quietly without much movement as if he had been told not to stir or else he would be punished. He did not make eye contact with him, no muscle moved on his face.

But after a while, he ran away into an interior room. Nasir had brought with him a red toy fire truck, which he had hidden in his pocket. He followed the quiet boy and offered it to him and beckoned him to come closer.

It was as if God had planned their union. Nasir reached for him and softly said, "Ayaan?" The child looked up and nodded quietly. He knelt beside the boy, laid him gently against his chest, murmuring tender words to him, promising that he would take him away that very day. The boy grabbed his hands and wouldn't let go. After about half an hour of holding his hands, Nasir wriggled his fingers free, only to have the child clutch them again.

Nasir took the boy's face in his hands and saw Nafisa in him. He had the same big, dark eyes with long eyelashes and the same nose. His heart ached with pity for the child, abandoned and left in this cheerless institution. No more. Nasir would make up for the lack of love that began this boy's life.

The search was finally over for Nasir, or at least half over, and he was delighted beyond measure.

As Nasir led him into the house, Ayaan's small feet slapped in loose flip-flops, his eyes trained to look down on the ground. He stood breathless before them and shrank into a corner of the room, leaning closely against the wall, trying to look small, as if to show them how very little space he required from them to shelter him.

"This is Ayaan, Ammu, Nafisa's son. He has come to live with us," Nasir introduced the little boy to his mother.

"To live with us?" she repeated in a hoarse voice. She grew pallid, like a corpse, and her face hardened into a scowl. "I can't believe you. Do you realize what you are doing? He is a child of shame and will bring shame upon our household."

"He is Nafisa's son," Nasir replied, taking the little boy's hand between his own palms. "That's all we need to know."

She turned to her husband, who was standing by her side. "Can you believe this? We won't be able to show our faces in town."

Nasir's father stayed quiet.

"Where else should my sister's child make his home?" Nasir reasoned. He watched his mother survey the boy from top to bottom. "He cannot help his birth. He is not to be blamed for being born. He is innocent. And he is of our blood."

She listened in silence, but her eyes burned, and her hands worked nervously around each other.

"He is certainly Nafisa's son, but you'll talk to me about this later," she murmured finally, breaking the silence between them.

In the ensuing month that followed, Nasir cut through rolls of bureaucratic red tape to make Ayaan a permanent part of their family. He knew the boy was in desperate need of exercise, mental stimulation, and lots of love, and his patience knew no end.

Ayaan refused to be touched by anyone. He was skittish, distrustful, and super sensitive to physical touch. Only his uncle could hold him, and he screamed if anybody other than Nasir approached him. Nasir took it all in stride—all the clinging and whining and night terrors—though his mother insisted he was spoiling the child. He let Ayaan climb on his knees and ride on his shoulders. He rocked him to sleep every night, as he pressed his small body into Nasir's and gathered fistfuls of his clothing in his small hands. Every day, Nasir told the boy how much he loved him.

Nasir noticed that his father was totally confused about how to treat his grandson. He knew his parents struggled to accept this "child of the enemy" as part of the family. But his father seemed particularly torn. The child's mere being extended their daughter's memory to the past and into the future. He was a living memory of the war and the terrible treatment their daughter had suffered and survived—but could never recover from. They had failed to protect Nafisa, and the shame was too great for his father to bear. He refrained from saying anything harsh to Nasir from a sense of fear—afraid of alienating his son on whom the whole household was dependent financially and emotionally. Nasir knew this inner conflict roiled inside his father but would not relent in his insistence they accept Ayaan.

One day, Nasir was encouraged when his father returned from the market and touched Ayaan's soft cheek.

"I have something for you today," his father said. Grinning, he produced a fat, ripe mango from his shopping bag. "Go ask your uncle to cut it for you."

But then Nasir sometimes overheard or walked into a room and saw him treating the child horribly. He would call him names, throw things at him, call him dumb, and sometimes even slap the boy.

At family gatherings, his cousins ignored him and refused to include him, looking as though his very presence was irksome.

One day, Nasir overheard the maid suspiciously whispering to Ayaan, "Who are you? Where have you come from?" She gave him a long, hard look and walked away.

He also observed that friends who came to visit them talked in constant, covert whispers. Neighbors gathered around to see the sudden emergence of a new kid in the neighborhood and looked upon him curiously.

Nasir saw two women in the neighborhood lock eyes on Ayaan. One of them whispered to the other, "His mother was one of *those* women."

"Do you speak to him in Bengali?" the woman asked Nasir with a contemptuous glance.

"He's a little over two," Nasir answered, squinting his eyes in confusion. "He's still too young for all that."

The woman nodded in affirmation.

The other woman turned to her friend. "I have a son his age. I shall make sure they never play together."

Though Nasir had not expected the transition to be easy, he was dismayed that the stubborn community seemed unable to accept his nephew. Within a few months, the neighbors all avoided them, then began to disrespect Nasir.

Nasir's mother took on a pinched countenance, her mouth puckered as if she'd bitten something sour. He knew she held back the words "I told you so" and that the bitter, unspoken statement sat on her tongue, distaste fomenting into deep resentment.

As years went by, Nasir saw more and more of his sister's image in Ayaan. He had never doubted this was her son, but now the similarities confirmed it. Everyone could see how remarkably he looked like her.

At ten years of age, the boy had the same mold of chin and brow, sunken dark eyes, and thick, black hair. But there was an inner turmoil so intense that it threatened to tear him apart. His nephew was a constant reminder of the horrors of war.

～

Ayaan loved his Uncle Nasir dearly. Uncle protected him staunchly and yet could not control what happened when he was away from the house. As soon as Uncle left for work, Grandmother and Grandfather gave him chores to do, slapping the back of his head if he moved too slowly. Often, he was asked to do household chores whilst his cousins went outside to play. He was made to clean up after every meal, do the dishes, and wash vegetables that they brought from the market.

At breakfast and lunch, he was given only leftover food. If any scraps remained.

"Eat those," his grandmother would say. "The maid doesn't care for them and there's no sense in wasting the food."

Uncle Nasir would be angry if he knew, but Ayaan never told him. They already had fights about Ayaan and he hated being the reason for them. Nasir pretended as if all was well. But Ayaan knew his family disliked him and that he was the cause of these fights between his uncle and his grandmother.

The children at school didn't like him either. Neither did his teachers. He was frequently dragged to the front of the classroom and laughed at when he could not answer questions correctly. His teachers never stopped the humiliation but stood and smirked as the other children jeered at him.

Worse even than the routine humiliation was the "teacher's stick." Sloppy handwriting, inability to work sums, or sometimes nothing at all prompted the teacher to reach for his stick. Ayaan did not speak about those incidents to his uncle, but Uncle Nasir noticed the marks when Ayaan changed clothes. Furious, he promised to go to the school the very next day, but Ayaan always begged him not to. He just wanted to be left alone.

He started wetting his bed, a new reason for Grandmother to be angry with him since she needed to wash his sheets almost every morning. The angrier she became, the worse he felt, and the more helpless he was to change anything. Every morning, he woke up, cold and wet, knowing she would berate him again. He cried bitterly on the way to school, nauseous with dread as he wondered what he would do today to incur the wrath of the teachers.

Ayaan had no reason to believe his life would ever change. He knew other children were not treated the same way but he didn't know what he had done. All he knew from the taunts of others was that his mother had done something. They called her terrible names.

One day, he didn't go home after school. Some of the boys had cornered him and been particularly vicious with their bullying, even pushing him down and kicking him. When Ayaan didn't fight back, they gave up and walked away, laughing. Ayaan could not take any more. Home would offer no comfort and school was miserable. He stood, brushed himself off, and walked away, no destination in mind. He said nothing to anyone, just simply kept walking, sure that nothing could be worse than going home.

And yet, he discovered he was wrong. Home at least had Uncle and a bed and some food. He wandered for days, determined to find his own way in the world. But everyone in their town knew who he was. He set off on the road out of town, no idea where it would take him. He slept little and ate less. He lasted only three days, then returned home, hungry and tired. Grandmother looked disappointed when he walked back in the door. But Uncle Nasir swooped upon him, lifting him from the ground in a crushing hug.

"Ayaan! Where have you been? I was worried sick."

"Please don't be angry with me," Ayaan pleaded. He didn't have the strength for punishment and longed to go to his bed.

"Never," Uncle said, rocking him gently. "You are my boy and this is your home. You belong, Ayaan."

Grateful for acceptance, Ayaan wished more people felt that way.

Eighteen

THE REUNION

Nafisa had settled into her solitary life and learned to find, if not joy, at least contentment. Her work occupied her days. Sometimes being all alone in her house weighed on her. But she was grateful for a home. She had been homeless and did not wish to go back.

Calcutta remained her home. She had not been back to Dhaka in decades and some days wondered if her family ever missed her. But so much time had passed. Besides, she could not bear being rejected again.

One day, a letter arrived for her. The unfamiliar handwriting confused her. A moment of panic accompanied the thought that perhaps her husband was finally coming back. But no, he had been so much older and surely his drinking did nothing to improve his life and prolong his life.

Nafisa carried the letter inside, her hands shaking. Something about the writing triggered long-buried memories. She sat down and opened the envelope. A photograph fluttered to the floor. A young man stared at her from the picture with eyes that seemed to stare into her soul. Her heart skipped a beat, the resemblance to her brother so startling. If someone had shown her this image and told her it was a photograph of Nasir as a young man, she would have believed them. She withdrew the accompanying handwritten letter:

> Dearest Nafisa,
>
> I have searched for you since the war ended. I wished for you to come home, but since you did not, I never stopped looking. Finally, I have found you. I would like to come see you but did not want to upset you by showing up unannounced.
>
> Nafisa, I have another surprise. I found Ayaan. He has lived with us since he was two. I would like to bring him to meet you, if you allow it. He has longed for you all these years.
>
> Your brother,
> Nasir

She stared at the photograph, at her child, and a cold shiver ran through her as she collapsed into a nearby chair. What she saw immediately was the striking resemblance between herself and the bold youth in the picture.

She immediately wrote back, agreeing to meet them both. But no sooner did it leave her home than she realized the gravity of the situation.

Ayaan would soon find out who he really was. She knew how it was going to hurt him when he came to know the truth of his parentage. She did not want her son to know, sure he would be better off in complete ignorance. How could she face him and acknowledge she had given him away? Yet, what else could she do? Fate had come to call, and she must meet it, whatever it may be. Perhaps she would now atone for her mistake. As she looked at the picture more intently, she saw anguish in the young man's eyes. What had his life been like? Could he ever forgive her for leaving him motherless?

But as days went by, her courage and strength increased, as did her curiosity. She caught her reflection in the discolored mirror and cringed a little. Her once smooth and jet-black hair was ragged, with white frayed hair threading through, as though she were unravelling. Wrinkles cracked her skin, reminding her of the passage of time. She could not allow Nasir or Ayaan to see her this way.

She paid more attention to her meals and took care with her grooming. Soon her gaunt looks and the lines of stress on her face disappeared. Her face brightened at the prospect of seeing her son. She straightened her home and cleaned thoroughly. She needed this connection. And then she realized that they both needed each other. She would spend the rest of her life making up for the lost time.

The day of Nasir's visit arrived. Low, thick clouds moved in, turning the sky gray at noon. The air was sticky and hot before the first patters of raindrops landed on the rough, stony ground. After the first few drops, warm southwest winds brought a deluge of cascading water, beating passionately against the casements of her small windows. The flowers in her garden were completely drenched, and their drooping, wet faces turned southward. She could barely hear her own thoughts without the soothing sound of perpetual rain flowing through her consciousness. She felt drowsy for a moment. How she would spend this rainy afternoon was predetermined. She was not to endure the storm in solitude; she was to keep calm with company.

A knock at the door startled her, though she expected it.

"Yes?" she called through the door.

"Is that you, Nafisa?"

She opened the door and looked upon her brother for the first time in over two decades. *He's so old*, she thought with a shock, forgetting that time would have worked on him exactly as it had her. Of course, her own reflection continued to surprise her. Where had the years gone? In her mind, the two of them remained as they had been.

"I've been looking for you for so many years." Nasir was clearly nervous. His eyes sought forgiveness.

She shook herself back to this moment and welcomed him inside. "How did you find me?"

"I discovered Afsana and Shiraj live nearby. They shared your whereabouts. I am glad you had friends to support you."

"Yes." She did not offer any additional details. The friendship between Afsana and Nafisa had stagnated and faded into the background for some time after Nafisa moved out. She'd married and made new friends, though none replaced Afsana in her heart. How had she allowed a foolish crush to destroy her closest friendship?

But then, Afsana had reached out, letting her know Razia missed her second mother. Nafisa was quick to respond, eager to repair the friendship. After all, she and Afsana had been friends since they were young girls. After that, they had grown closer, best friends once again, though perhaps not as they once had been, the ugliness tainting their memories never completely wiped away. But she cherished the friendship and she had spent time with Razia as she grew, as her Auntie—

"You do not seem to be happy to see me, Nafisa," Nasir said.

"No, I am so happy to see you." Nafisa collected herself, pushing aside all other thoughts. "Come inside. I'll make tea."

"It is like old times to be here, but you've changed profoundly through the years," he said, as he hugged his sister.

"Ah, old times. I wish we could return to the old times, before the war. That was another life, though. You're a different person now, as am I. We knew peace and comfort back then, but we can't restore the years we've missed."

"If I had seen a little bit more clearly in the past, the things that happened to you could have been avoided. I shouldn't have

left home to fight the war." He choked up, tears filling his eyes.
"I have wanted to apologize for so long."

"You had no choice, Nasir, and I never once blamed you.
There is nothing to forgive."

He opened his arms, and she hugged him. Despite what she
said about not needing an apology, something shifted deep
inside. Perhaps just hearing the words made all the difference.

Nasir dried his eyes. "I did not come here to talk about the
war and bring back unhappy memories. What's done is done. I
came here to see you and stand by your side and to tell you that
you will never want for anything. If you ever need anything, let
me know."

"I don't need anything now," she said. "Yes, I struggled for
many years. But life has a way of giving me what I need. Sometimes in very strange ways. But here I am, and I am okay. And it
feels good to stand up on my own feet. I don't need anyone."

"You can come and stay with us now," he said. "I brought
Ayaan home and now I can bring you home too. No one will say
a word against you. Not while I'm around."

"There have been times when I would have given anything in
the world to be able to go back to our old home and you, but
that is not my home anymore," Nafisa replied.

"Nafisa," he said imploringly, "I want so badly to make things
right."

She placed a hand on his cheek. "I know you mean well. But
we can only go forward, not back. And I will not go back to a
place that rejected me. My life is here now."

"I think I understand," he said, though he sounded disappointed. "Or at least, I accept it. I am so proud of you. You were
always so strong."

Nafisa remembered how helpless she had been to stop the
soldiers, how they had taken her by force. How her own mother
had looked upon her in disdain and refused to let her come
home. The refugee camps. Taking refuge with Afsana and Shiraj
only to destroy that opportunity. She did not feel strong. She felt

battered and worn down and weary. Her memories of being a student at Dhaka University seemed like a dream, something that happened to someone else, someone who had a bright future.

"I do not wish to talk about the past anymore, Nasir. Let's talk about something good. Tell me about Ayaan," she said.

"Ayaan is ready to meet you. I told him about you," he said. "But I did not bring him today. I worried both of us might be too much at once."

She took a deep breath. "I am ready. I want to know my son."

Despite Nafisa's extreme eagerness to finally be reunited with her child, a week passed before they returned to Calcutta.

It was late in the evening when they arrived.

Nafisa's stomach twisted into knots when she heard the knock on the door. When she opened it, she stared in disbelief. Her son was now something real and tangible. She had not known what to expect in this moment, but her heart gave a leap.

She was given an opportunity to seize a second chance of becoming a mother to him. The face she had wondered about all these years—it was suddenly there in front of her.

And on his face, she saw her own features. Somehow, though he had never known her, his mannerisms and gestures were like hers. She pressed her hand upon her heart as if to silence its painful throbs, whilst she devoured every line of his face, tracing his handsome features to etch them in her memory.

Nafisa tried to speak but could not utter a word. She reached out and gently stroked his cheek.

Suddenly, with a soft cry, she pulled her son to her.

He clasped his arms around her, and they held onto one another in a long and close embrace. Every breath seemed to be full of love, immersed in the speechless joy that permits no words. Every few seconds they pulled back and just stared at each other, both crying and smiling and laughing.

Finally, Nafisa whispered, "Ayaan, my beautiful boy."

"He looks just like you, Nafisa," Nasir said.

"Yes, I can see."

Ayaan turned to his mother. "Ammu," he said, "where have you been?"

Nafisa paused, thinking carefully about what to say. She spoke truthfully. "I have been lost, chasing things that were not meant for me."

Ayaan, unsatisfied with her answer, began firing more questions. "Tell me why I was torn away from you. Why will no one tell me who my father is? What is this terrible mystery?"

"Not yet, my son," she almost whispered. "I will tell you everything one day, but not now. Let's not spoil this moment."

"You know I love you, Ammu. I have loved you for years."

Fresh tears filled her eyes. "I will never forgive myself for giving you up. But I have no doubt that God has accepted my suffering as an atonement, since he has brought back my son to me."

"Don't distress yourself, Ammu. I am not here to judge you or demand an explanation. Uncle and I are here to help you."

As happy as she was, there followed an interval of acute anxiety. Nafisa's tendency to internalize her suffering caused her to refrain from telling anybody about her reunion with her son. She stayed aloof throughout and did not share the news with anyone, not even Afsana and Shiraj.

Nineteen

TIME DISCOVERS THE TRUTH

As the years rolled by, everything seemed to be perfect in Afsana's life. Despite a few bumps, she and Shiraj were close and happy. Her daughter Razia had a wonderful childhood. They had everything they needed and some things they wanted.

One point of contention was that Afsana had never shared with Razia who her biological father was. Afsana saw no reason to divulge this information. She never saw the need to bring up the past or to potentially shatter Razia's firm foundation. Shiraj had been the perfect father. He was the only father Razia had ever known. He showered her with all the attention, stability, and unconditional love of a devoted father. As far as Afsana was concerned, he was Razia's true father.

Shiraj, on the other hand, had often asked his wife to reveal the truth, to be upfront with their daughter about the circumstances.

"From a medical standpoint, it is the logical approach," he told her on several occasions. "What if she needs to know about a genetic condition she could be carrying from her biological father?"

Afsana brushed the idea away, knowing she had no way of

determining any genetics involved. "Whatever happens to Razia, you and I will care for her. So what difference does it make?"

When Razia was twelve, he pushed the issue.

"It's time to tell her the truth. You ought to be honest about her real father. We mustn't hide this from our daughter. Imagine how she will feel if she learns this information from someone other than us. One day she will surely discover the truth."

"Shiraj, she is too young," Afsana replied. "Just let her lead a happy childhood."

"When the truth comes out, she will be angry with us. If she comes to know at an earlier age, she will be able to cope with it psychologically, and eventually, she'll prefer knowing to not knowing," Shiraj insisted.

"I will wait until she is old enough to understand the complexities of the situation. We should not exasperate Razia with knowledge she cannot handle. Right now she lacks the maturity. How will she feel to learn you are not her biological father? For now, let me raise her in a beautiful bubble of innocence as long as possible. So far, it has worked out well for us. When the time comes, she'll know and will accept it."

But when Razia turned fifteen, she began to ask questions.

"Ammu, do you miss your father sometimes?" she asked her mother, rather out of nowhere.

"I do miss my parents. War takes many things from us, Razia."

"I want to hear more about my grandfather."

Afsana told stories from her youth, of her father carrying her on his shoulders, lifting her to pluck mangoes from the tree in their back yard, holding her on his lap. "Just like your Abbu."

"And who do you think you resemble most, grandmother or grandfather?"

"Oh, I don't know. I never gave it much thought. Why do you ask?"

"The other day my music teacher made a comment. She says I look nothing like my father. Do you look like your father?"

A cloud fell on Afsana's face. She would have some choice words for this music teacher. Who did she think she was to stir up trouble like this?

"Of course, Razia, you are the true image of your father."

"But my friends tell me I don't look like my father, too."

Afsana forced a smile for her daughter. "I have always been delighted that you look exactly like me. Don't you agree? Perhaps my genes are stronger. Just tell them your mother's dominant genetics won this time."

When Razia asked no further questions and seemed satisfied for the time being, Afsana breathed a sigh of relief, as though she had dodged a bullet aiming for her heart.

But Razia was not satisfied. She knew her mother carried a secret, something no one would share with her. From a young age, she had heard her mother cry out in the night, then heard Father comfort her. She did not know why she was crying, but she thought her Ammu was having bad dreams, and that it must have been something very frightening. She tried to get back to sleep by burying her head under her pillow so she would not have to hear her mother crying.

When Razia asked her father about her mother's cries at night, the furrow of her father's brow indicated he did not wish to talk about it. But the unknown allowed Razia's imagination to run away, and she became convinced something was wrong with her mother. Eventually, Abbu confirmed she suffered from nightmares, and that her mind was still tortured by the painful memories of the war.

Razia did not know what exactly her mother was dreaming about the war, or what the war really was, because it was never discussed. The war was a mysterious thing, spoken of only in whispers and hidden from her all her life. She was determined to find out why her mother was so upset that she suffered ongoing nightmares.

Razia began to pry about it, and her quest for answers continued. Family secrets have a way of being felt even if they're unspoken. She always had a sense that something was not as it seemed.

Razia approached Auntie Nafisa about it. She knew her mother had been friends with Auntie since they were little girls. Perhaps she would be able to answer her questions.

One day when Auntie came to visit, Razia drew her aside and spoke with her quietly.

"There's something on my mind that's been driving me crazy. And I think you'll be the right person to answer my question."

Auntie Nafisa frowned. "If something is bothering you, you should ask your mother. She would want to be the one to talk with you, Razia."

"I have tried to ask her and Abbu. They won't talk to me. Surely you know something. You've known each other for a long time."

"What is it that's bothering you?"

"Ammu has terrible nightmares. Abbu says it's from the war. Do you know what happened to her during the war?"

"I don't know if I should talk about it." Auntie Nafisa shifted uncomfortably. "Not me. Not yet."

"But I hear her crying out in the night and it scares me."

"This is not for me to share, Razia. Your Ammu will tell you everything you need to know. If she ever decides to tell you."

"But maybe I could—"

"You can never understand what we went through. It is impossible to forget. I have nightmares too."

She took Auntie Nafisa's hands in both of her own. "Please, no one talks about it. Surely talking about it would be better than keeping everything secret."

Auntie Nafisa closed her eyes. "It is a sad tale, and one which would re-open wounds in your mother's heart, long closed by now."

"But they aren't closed, are they? Not if she is plagued by nightmares."

"Have you heard of the *birangona* in school? Your mother and I were taken as prisoners during the war, kept in cells for months. We were starved and mistreated. I will spare you the details, Razia. Suffice it to say we were tortured. The memories plague us."

"I guessed as much, and I feared it," Razia answered.

"Worst of all . . ." Auntie Nafisa seemed on the verge of sharing something critical, but then seemed to change her mind. "Worst of all we were rejected by our families after the war ended, considered tainted by the hands of the enemy. Please don't ask me anything more, Razia. I have said all I can say."

Though her mind spun vivid images of her mother as a prisoner of war, Razia remained unsatisfied and tried another approach.

"How did you meet my mother and father?"

At this, Auntie Nafisa seemed to brighten. "Your mother and I grew up together of course. And then went to Dhaka University together. Those are some of the best memories of my life, before the war, when we all thought liberation would come without sacrifice. My brother Nasir and I were best friends with your mother and Farzad—"

Auntie clapped her hands over her mouth and her eyes went wide. Somewhere deep in Razia's psyche, a memory stirred. She focused on the memory, coaxing it out of hiding until she could just remember.

"When I was little, I was lost at the fair and could not find my way back to my mother. A man discovered me alone and scared. I remember him asking, 'Are you lost, my little one? I'll help you find your Ammu.' He took my hand and helped me find her. He even gave me some beautiful glass bangles. I remember Ammu went to the fair several times to see him again. Whenever she met him, she was very sad, and cried every night in her bed after she came home. I had completely forgotten until you said the name, but Ammu called him Farzad."

"Are you certain that was the name?"

"Yes. He was scarred and seemed unable to remember Ammu. But she spoke to him as if they knew each other."

"I don't know if I should tell you this. Farzad was her first husband, but I thought he was dead. We thought he died in the war. Afsana never talked about finding Farzad." Auntie Nafisa looked a little offended for being left in the dark.

The knowledge her mother had been married to someone other than her Abbu shook Razia more deeply than learning she had been a prisoner of war. For the first time in her life, Razia felt a distance between her mother and her, as if her mother were speaking to her from a place thousands of miles away. But she did not blame her for keeping her secrets.

Afsana noticed a distance between her and Razia but attributed it to her daughter gaining independence. In fact, she considered the young woman too independent. Now that she was twenty, marriage proposals were pouring in, but Razia had no interest in them. Suitors, like bees, swarmed about her as she blossomed into a beautiful flower. She worried herself constantly, concerned with nothing as much as ensuring her daughter would marry someone suitable, someone who could give her a good life.

To her dismay, Razia began to talk about someone she met through a friend. This brought back memories of her own mother, and how she, too, wanted Afsana to marry someone of her parents' choice. But she had pushed to choose for herself and marry Farzad. *And just look how that turned out*, Afsana thought. She would save Razia from herself, save her from the sort of heartache she had endured by marrying for love.

MY WAR, MY CHILD · 153

"Ammu, once and for all, I can never marry someone I do not love. I will not marry for money and if I ever marry at all—"

"You wish to live in poverty all your life?" Afsana asked. "I have experienced that. Trust me, you could not handle it."

"You and Abbu always make the decisions for me. That was fine when I was young. But I am a grown woman now and can think for myself. After all, I think that, regarding important matters of the heart, everybody should make their own decisions."

Out of nowhere, Shiraj made a sudden appearance. "True, my child. I also chose love over all else." Shiraj beamed at Afsana.

But Afsana didn't want to be wooed, she wanted to be supported. The memory of her husband defying his parents to marry her may have sounded romantic, but the truth was they had no extended family as a result.

"How can you allow her to make this huge decision without us? Poor decisions tarnish the reputation of a young woman and her family. She is too young. Young people make wrong choices."

She covered her face with both hands and slid into a chair.

Shiraj knelt beside her. "But, my love, just look at us. Everyone told us we would be miserable. And here we are."

"We were far more mature, Shiraj. War forced us to grow up fast."

"Razia is more sheltered, sure, but she is an intelligent young woman."

Afsana would not be swayed, however, and continued to prepare an arranged marriage for her daughter. One of her friends was an excellent matchmaker in their community. She entrusted her daughter's future to the woman.

Her friend accepted with unprecedented enthusiasm. She rushed in one day and announced that the groom that she had been talking about should be taken into consideration. She also emphasized that this marriage would benefit Razia's long-term future. The young man's present income, overall social status, and reputation of his family were excellent.

Afsana called for Razia, who was in the dark as far as these plans went.

"We have found your match! He is a good man with whom your future would be secure. He'll be able to protect you from all dangers," Afsana told her daughter.

"You want me to marry a stranger? A man I don't love?" Razia asked.

"Yes, my dear child. I am arranging for happiness for the rest of your life. Not a few bright years of infatuation followed by misery."

Shiraj frowned.

"But . . . I love someone else! How can I marry this man when my heart belongs to another?"

"You . . . love somebody?"

"Yes, I love someone else with all my heart."

"Have you no shame? Confessing your love for another man as your mother tells you about your marriage match? I had no idea you've been seeing someone!"

Embarrassed, the matchmaker excused herself and left.

"I told you I met someone. Do you care about my happiness at all?" Razia asked.

"I do understand, far better than you, child," replied her mother. "You have no idea what life is about or what could be waiting in your future."

"You only care for a life of ease, with a grand house, servants, all that money can buy. But I care nothing for these. I want love and happiness," Razia replied.

"You will care about a life of ease the first time your stomach rumbles with hunger and your pantry is bare! Love and happiness! There is no such love in this world. There are loves that end in disaster. The world is strewn with such. And why do you think these loves go astray? Because they went contrary to the will of their parents."

"Afsana—" Shiraj tried to intervene.

"Love does exist!" Razia stamped her foot like a child.

"Hush!" said her mother almost fiercely, and then she broke into a scornful laugh. "What do you know about the frailties and inconsistency of human love? It is transient, the most unreal, like a shimmering bubble."

"Razia," Shiraj interrupted, "please allow me to speak with your mother alone."

Razia nodded and went to her own room.

"Do you know how many girls would jump at the chance to marry this young man? And she throws it away as if it were nothing! For what? A silly dream!"

"Afsana, do you truly feel love is nothing but a silly dream?"

Expecting an argument about Razia, Afsana stood silent, caught off guard.

Shiraj looked crushed. "And to think, all these years I believed we found the love and happiness that Razia describes. Perhaps it has been one-sided all along. Your love apparently ended in disaster."

"Shiraj, no. Please forgive me. I spoke in anger." She went to his side and embraced him. "You are my true love. Farzad is the one that ended in disaster. He was my choice. My parents had made a match for me, and I refused. Look what happened."

Shiraj's eyes softened, and he took her hand. "My love, what happened set you on a path to me. I know you have been through terrible things. I wish I could take away the lingering pain and distress. But I would not change a thing about your past. Because everything that happened to you brought you to me."

"Oh, Shiraj." Afsana collapsed against him. "I do love you. Truly."

"Ammu?" Razia appeared quite suddenly. "Who is Farzad?"

"Razia! Were you listening? I asked for privacy," Shiraj said.

"It's okay," Afsana said and took a deep breath. "Razia has a right to know the truth. I waited too long. Come and sit, my child."

Clutching tightly to Shiraj's hand for support, Afsana shared the most painful memories of her life with her daughter and husband. She held back the darkest moments, but shared how she met Farzad, their involvement in the liberation movement, and how her parents agreed to their wedding.

"Your Aunt Nafisa and her brother Nasir were at our wedding. But then everything fell apart. Perhaps if I had married the man the matchmaker had found for me, I would never have been taken prisoner, targeted as Farzad's wife." Of course, even as she said this, she realized what she was saying—that wishing for a different life meant wishing this one away. "I hope you do not see me any differently. I do not want anyone's pity."

"I would not change one thing," Shiraj repeated. "I love you as you are."

"Ammu, don't wish your life away. Thank you for finally being honest with me. At least now I can understand why this is so important to you." Razia took a deep breath. "If you think it is right for me to marry the man of your choice, I will agree. But know that I will be marrying one man while loving another."

Twenty

THE CHILDREN OF WAR

The first time Razia met Ayaan, he filled her heart, as if some missing piece had finally clicked into place. They were in the same class, but she could not focus on the professor at all, so taken with this boy he completely distracted her. And though he fixed his eyes on the front of the classroom, every few minutes he would turn his eyes her way. But she would look away.

Eventually, he turned toward her and smiled. Razia could see that his life had not been one of indolence and ease. He had a thoughtful brow, where lines deepened his features. His face was bronzed with extreme exposure, so she knew he worked. His sharp nose slightly deviated to the left, hinting at an injury sometime in the past. But his face harmonized perfectly well with his figure.

After class, Razia asked her friend who he was.

"Oh, haven't you met him before? That is Ayaan. He's friends with my brother. Come here!" She grabbed Razia's hand and dragged her to where the boy stood. "Salam, Ayaan! This is my friend Razia."

They saw each other routinely after that, and three months later he asked her on a date. They kept their conversation casual.

He had worn his military uniform, which she found quite dashing.

"Your father must be so proud and happy that you're home from training," she could not help remarking.

He went silent and his face grew a shade paler.

"I am sorry. I did not mean to pry."

"No, it's okay. It's just . . . my uncle raised me."

"That's nothing to be ashamed of," Razia said.

"I'm not. I'm not ashamed to talk about him."

"You seem upset about something."

Ayaan sighed. "I have never met my father. I don't know who he is. I only met my mother recently and learned she was the victim of an assault during the war. I was the result of that assault. She gave me up for adoption, but my uncle found me in the orphanage and took me home."

"That wasn't your doing," Razia said. "You have no reason to—"

"My entire life, I was teased and tormented. Heard my mother called a whore. Got into fights when I got older." He touched his nose. "So I understand if you're disgusted and don't want to see me again."

Razia caught her breath. "I would never judge you for this. Your mother was a victim of the war. I am appalled to hear how you were treated. How could anyone treat a child that way?"

Ayaan lifted his eyes to meet her gaze. "You mean that sincerely?"

"From my heart," she assured him.

He reached across the table and took her hand.

She thrilled to his touch and smiled warmly. "I hope we will see more of each other."

Through the balmy spring, and the hot months of summer, they spent every possible moment together. Razia had heard stories of rapturous love that caused restlessness and sleepless nights, loss of appetite, a constant need to be with each other.

But what she felt for Ayaan was simpler than that, plain and straightforward.

It was not until Ayaan came to tell her he had received a new assignment and would soon leave that Razia realized how dearly she loved him.

Just before he left, they met again. He invited her to a secluded part of a park, where they sat beneath the shadow of a banyan tree. A strange timidity overwhelmed her as both of them avoided discussing his imminent departure. But finally she brought it up.

"I am glad that we could see each other before you leave, even if it is for a short while," she told him, taking his hand and holding it in hers.

"It will be for a short time only," he said, wiping away her sad tears.

"Always remember that I am here for you. Anytime you are afflicted with bad memories of your childhood or feel that you are all alone, find comfort in the thought that I love you," Razia replied.

"I will try to do so, Razia," he said. "I love you, too."

"I feel as if we were destined to meet, and I hope that in the future we can walk the same path together. I wish you did not have to leave."

"Sometimes I reproach myself for the wrong I have done to you." His voice had a note in it, a touch of bitterness, which surprised her.

"In what way have you wronged me?" she asked him.

"I have wronged you by forcing myself upon you," he replied. "I have been selfish, eagerly spending time with you when you deserve so much better. I hoped to win your heart but how can I ever claim it? I am poor and friendless. Your parents will never view me as a good match. They will never approve of me."

Razia laughed, though his drawn face clearly conveyed his agony. He truly believed himself worthless, and that broke her heart. "No, Ayaan, you didn't force yourself on me. I was drawn to you, from the moment we first met. Why wouldn't it make me proud and happy if you were to come to me and ask me to share your life with you?"

"But your parents—"

"My parents married for love. Abbu will understand and he will convince Ammu. They were not an arranged match. I know they will support us."

Ayaan's voice quavered. "I can hardly dare to hope for such a treasure as you to be mine. The thought will see me through until I can return to you."

Twenty-One

AN UNFINISHED BUSINESS

As Razia's wedding day drew closer, Afsana noticed her daughter becoming more and more withdrawn. She suspected it was because of the boy she had met and claimed to love. This was not how she had imagined wedding preparations for her only daughter. She had imagined them chatting and laughing, choosing just the right dress and planning the perfect celebration. But Razia had no interest in the preparations. Anytime Afsana asked her opinion, her morose daughter responded, "I don't care. You can choose." She missed the deep connection the two had always enjoyed but remained convinced that eventually Razia would see this was for the best and be grateful.

During one solitary trip to the market, which Razia had declined to accompany her on, Afsana felt as though she were being watched. She would turn around to look but found no one tailing her.

Her search for a wedding outfit for herself led her to a rather quiet part of the market, where fewer people mingled between the vendors' stalls. This time when she turned around, she came face to face with a young man.

"Are you following me?" she asked.

The young man didn't say anything. Instead, he handed her a note.

"Who is this from?" she asked.

"Don't know, I was told to give it to you." He turned and left.

Afsana unfolded the paper.

Afsana,

I know that it's been a long time and you weren't expecting to hear from me. I am in Calcutta now, please meet me tomorrow at noon at the fairgrounds.

Farzad

A mixture of excitement and fear burned in her as she held the note in her trembling hands. She began to battle with herself, allowing herself to be guided by both conscience and reason. What was the line that would determine that this was an inappropriate meeting? She knew a wrong decision on her part, whatever it was, would seal her fate forever.

She didn't tell Shiraj about Farzad's note because she didn't want to worry him. She loved her husband deeply and nothing could threaten that. But she was rather curious to find out the reason for this unexpected visit. She argued with herself back and forth as she contemplated what to do.

What good is he going to do to me now? He left me behind once and then sent me away. What could he possibly want? Razia is getting married, I don't want any distractions in my life at this moment. Afsana decided she would not go.

But her feet dragged her to the fairground at the appointed time. The same fairground where she had encountered him so many years ago.

Afsana waited for him and began to wonder if this was all an elaborate hoax to once again humiliate her. But he arrived, still limping, and their eyes met.

The years of history flooded back, and she wondered if she should open or slam shut her heart. It felt like they could pick up where they left off, but how could they possibly do that without getting hurt? And hurting others. Shiraj's face swam into her mind's eye. And that was all she saw.

Farzad was grayer and thinner, his eyes full of curiosity. With a smile on his face, he walked toward her, hands outstretched. He appeared much happier than the last time she'd seen him.

After a few moments of awkward silence, he put an arm around her shoulders as they strolled along the street looking for a place to sit and talk.

"Afsana, it's been a long, long time since I have seen you."

"A long time indeed, but not as long as I expected since I didn't think I would ever see you again."

"You sound angry."

She did not answer.

"What is it?" he said, with one of those rare smiles that made his handsome face look once again young and winsome. He took her hand in his, but she pulled it away.

"No, Farzad," she said. "I am another man's wife."

He gripped her hand tightly and bent his head nearer to her. "But you were my wife when you married him. Not free to marry at all."

"You know I believed you had been killed in the war. And when I came to you, you sent me away," Afsana said.

"I was wrong to be angry with you the day you came to see me in Dhaka," he said. "Say you forgive me, Afsana."

"There's nothing to forgive," answered Afsana.

"Then you will forgive me?"

"If that is what you came to hear, then yes, I have forgiven you. Things happened that were out of our control. We cannot be held accountable for them."

The two strode in silence, side by side, their distorted black shadows dancing grotesquely on the ground. They passed several more streets and decided to sit in a quieter place where they could talk without noise from the street. Walking a little farther, they found Calcutta Coffee House. They seated themselves next to each other on a discolored, padded bench in a far corner of the room.

A waiter walked briskly to their small table and handed them a menu.

He ordered their coffee and asked her if she would like something to eat. But Afsana declined. Coffee with an old friend seemed less formal than having a meal alone with another man.

Farzad looked around. "This reminds me of our nights at Madhur's Canteen."

As the memories flooded back and Afsana's heart threatened to let him back in, she agreed. But decided it was time to get to the point. "Farzad, I almost didn't come. Will you tell me why you sent the note? Why are we here?"

He took out a square-shaped paper box and handed it to Afsana. "These are for you and Razia," he said and smiled tenderly.

Afsana's hand trembled a little as she opened the box and peered into it—and gazed silently at the rows of colorful glass bangles. She lowered her head to hide the tears pooling in her eyes.

The waiter returned with their coffee. Afsana forced a smile as she accepted her cup. She sipped the hot brew, unable to look at Farzad. Why had she come? This was a terrible mistake, accomplishing nothing but opening old wounds.

"Are you feeling unwell?" Farzad asked.

"What is it that you want, Farzad?"

"Forget and forgive the past. Give me back your love and be my wife again. I did leave you once, and I deserve your distrust. And yes, I was rude, brutally rude, when you came to see me. I was selfish, very selfish, avoided all responsibilities when my memories returned. I know I am no hero, but I also know you are the only woman I have ever loved. And you once promised to love me forever."

"You ask for the impossible, Farzad. You are suggesting I throw my whole life away to come running back to you. You are still being selfish. Now that we are older and you don't want to be alone, you decide you love me and I am worth your time? No."

"I have never stopped loving you in all these years."

"Then where have you been, Farzad? Where were you when soldiers came beating on my door? Where were you when they shot my father and took him away? Where were you when they dragged me from my home, intent on holding me in your stead? And where were you when the war ended and I was alone and starving in the refugee camp?"

"I should have been there, I know. But remember I was badly injured too."

She regretted losing her temper and speaking the words she had kept to herself for decades. What good would these accusations do? It was all in the past, lost to history. Their chance had come and gone. "I know. I know you were. As I said, circumstances were out of our control."

"Let's keep in touch," he suggested. "We can meet every couple of weeks. We can rebuild our friendship first."

Afsana saw Shiraj's face and knew how much this would hurt him. "No. I cannot see you again."

"Why not?"

"How can I trust you again, Farzad?" she said. "And how can I trust myself around you?"

"I would rather have you in my life as a friend than not have you in my life at all. If you cannot be my wife, at least be my friend. I cannot live without you."

"You have lived without me all these years just fine," she reminded him. "I don't know what has prompted this, but you will be okay."

She slowly rose from her seat, ready to leave. There was nothing for her here.

Farzad stood and grabbed her wrist. "When are you coming back to me, Afsana?"

"I just said I am not. And I don't think we should ever see each other again," she replied.

"You cannot mean that. Look me in the eye and tell me you don't love me."

She met his gaze levelly, unwaveringly. "I love Shiraj. I will always regret what happened to us, but what's done is done. We can complete the paperwork to formalize our separation."

"You can't . . . you don't mean that," he said.

"Yes, I mean that. We should have done it long ago. You will also be free to marry again, once it is final."

"I will never marry again," he said coldly. "I love only you."

"So be it. That is your decision."

"Then you never loved me," Farzad said. "Otherwise, you would love me still."

"I would argue you didn't love me. A person who loves you truly will never let you go whatever the situation is. You didn't have the courage to stand and fight for me. And it was Shiraj who picked up the pieces and gave me a life back. He was there when I had nothing."

His face fell. "That's a terrible thing to say," he muttered. His face reddened.

"It is the truth. Now I must hurry home now to Shiraj, who is waiting for me patiently."

Farzad sat back down. All the life seemed to drain out of him.

She picked up the bangles and started to leave but hesitated. "Thank you for the bangles. Razia is getting married soon. Perhaps she would like to wear them on her wedding day."

"Razia is all grown up and ready to be married? I miss her sometimes. I should have been part of her life. Another regret. But if she will wear them, her father will be with her in spirit at least on her wedding day. Unless you would permit me to come to the wedding?"

Afsana's blood ran cold. She froze in place. "What are you talking about?"

"She was six years old when you and I met again, was she not? The math is simple. We must have conceived her the night I visited you, before I went into hiding." He seemed to think of something new. "Perhaps she would like to spend time with her father. I have not been there, but I will be there now."

The secret that had plagued her for so many years rose to torment her yet again. "Do not interfere in this, Farzad."

"I have a right to see my daughter. And she has a right to know her true father."

"Farzad, Razia is not your daughter," Afsana whispered.

"What do you mean?" He jerked back. "I assumed . . . but you couldn't have met Shiraj until . . ." He pulled away, eyes widening.

She looked away, nausea percolating the coffee in her stomach.

"And your husband, how did Shiraj react to the fact that Razia is not his daughter? You were with someone else's child when he met you? How did you explain that?"

"Shiraj welcomed me in his arms and helped me the whole time. He is a good husband and a good father," she replied. "And he never demanded to know who the father was."

It was mostly true, though he had assumed Farzad was the baby's father. And in that moment, she realized how very deeply she loved Shiraj. Loved the husband he had been to her and the father he had been to Razia. No part of her longed for the thrilling excitement of youthful infatuation. Shiraj had loved her truly, with maturity and solidness and real love.

Farzad made no answer, but his face began to change, to darken a shade deeper.

He stood there like a man who was lost, an explicit contempt written all over his face. When he looked up, it was with a decision in his eyes.

With a hastened goodbye, he left her. Long after he was gone, she stood where he had left her, the feeling of wounded pride so strong within her that she could hardly endure it. Again, she gave away to a violent burst of tears.

This would be the last encounter with Farzad. Every time she thought she had forgotten him, he glided back into her life, unsettling her, challenging her love and admiration for Shiraj. And now this time reminding her of how Razia came to exist.

At home, she discovered Shiraj waiting rather impatiently for her to return from shopping. He looked a trifle sullen.

"I am back! You must have been worrying that I was lost," she said breathlessly.

He looked relieved as she entered. "So, you bought the whole store? Did you get something for yourself to wear on the wedding day?"

He threw himself without ceremony into an armchair and stretched out his slender legs. She gazed around her and smiled a nervous smile, unable to look him in the eye.

"I don't know. I didn't find anything I liked. Maybe Razia can help me find something another time."

A thousand fears chased each other through her head as she saw his forehead furrow. Despite her uneasiness, she talked to him with an easy tone, determined to appear calm. Shiraj's eyes never left her face, and there was a sudden splash of suspicion in his eyes as he held her gaze. She stiffened when he rose from his chair and approached her.

"My dear, you look quite agitated."

She sighed. After a moment's hesitation, she opted for complete honesty.

"While I was out, someone approached me with a note. It was from Farzad, asking me to meet him."

Shiraj's furrowed brow turned into a frown. "And did you?"

She dropped her gaze and nodded.

"I don't understand why he comes here like a sneaking thief, seeing you secretly, avoiding me. I'm not going to assault him! He can very well come to our house, sit with us, and have a hearty talk."

Afsana shrugged. "I don't understand it either."

Her calm and good-natured husband was more agitated than she had ever seen him. "And what did he want?"

"To talk." She twisted her hands together.

"That he could do here, in front of me. The insolence astonishes me. A man with any principle, any honor, would not continue to skulk back and harass you. And yet you meet him in secret and won't tell me what he said."

"But, Shiraj, there isn't much to tell except that we argued and fought most of the time." She began to feel beads of sweat gathering at her brow. Her emotional state was already fragile. She did not think she could bear another argument.

"And what did you argue about? What is the unfinished business that keeps bringing him back and that he cannot speak about in front of your husband?"

"He asked if we could be friends again."

"You gave me your word that you'd never see him again, and yet I find out he's trying to make his way back into your life. If he wants you back, he'll come to you saying all the right things to melt your heart."

"I don't see why I am being blamed for his coming back into my life when I really never wished to set eyes on him again."

"You could have told him no!"

"Don't raise your voice to me, Shiraj. And I was just telling Farzad how calm and gentle you are."

"I do not understand your fixation with him. Why do you refuse to let him go?"

"I told him repeatedly that I didn't want to see him again, and that our daughter was getting married in a short period of time."

"So you wish him to be at her wedding? As her father? Where has he been all her life?"

Afsana moved closer and touched his arm.

"It's nothing like that, Shiraj. Please. You are Razia's father." She covered her face, frustrated he would not believe her.

Shiraj leaned back in his chair. "Afsana, you cannot love me and Farzad. One of us must give way to the other."

"I don't want Farzad."

"But you love him," replied Shiraj.

"I love only you. Hear me, Shiraj, and believe me. The attachment I once had for Farzad still remains as a memory and always will. He was the first to awaken in me any real feeling."

"So you do still have feelings for him," he said.

"I have only the memories of feelings. You came into my life as a blessing, and I thank you for everything you've done for me. I am so dependent on you, you're so necessary to me, why, if you were to leave my life now, most of me would go with you. I promise you I would never take Farzad back even if he were to go down on his knees and beg me to be with him again. In fact, I . . . I told him today that I want to formalize our separation. He left quite angry with me." She gave his arm a little squeeze between her two clinging hands.

"You told him this?"

"I did. You are the only one for me, Shiraj. I love you."

"Thank you." Shiraj put his own hands upon hers. "But I wish you hadn't told him about Razia getting married. As her father, he may wish to be present. And after all, he really has nothing to do with her or the marriage and would only make things awkward."

It was as if he had a premonition about the coming event.

Twenty-Two

THERE'S A LIGHT TO BE FOUND

Time slipped by rapidly. The days grew into a week, then a fortnight, and then it was Razia's big day.

Wedding preparations were in full swing. Everything was coming together exactly as it was planned, regardless of certain disruptions in their lives.

Afsana worried and fretted, sometimes experiencing sudden attacks of anxiety and an overwhelming fear of unknown calamity. It was her beloved daughter Razia's wedding, and she had been waiting eagerly for this moment. She could not bear it if anything went wrong.

The event began perfectly, a lovely summer evening toward the close of the day, just between the light and the dark. The sky had mellowed, and the sun was setting, casting a muted golden light about them.

Silhouettes of flocks of birds streaked across the sky. The grazing herd of cows returned home from the pastures in the subdued light, eager to be with their calves. And the tinkling sound of the tiny bells around their necks gave intimation of their return. The loose red dust along the uneven roads, stirred up by their hooves, formed red clouds in the air.

The magical hour of *godhuli bela* (dusk) had always been regarded as an auspicious time for Bengali weddings.

Wasn't it the same one dusky evening when Afsana and Farzad tied the knot?

From where she sat near the window, Afsana gazed at the last sunbeams fading slowly, painting the sky shades of red and pink. The faint threads of red rays fell languidly on the curtains of the windows, announcing the end of a glorious day and the beginning of a new one.

There were stalwart men and youth amongst the guests bursting forth with laughter and merriment. She and Shiraj had been determined to give their daughter a lavish wedding, the grandest they could manage.

The room was filled with flowers, the air heavy with their perfume, and the sweet strains of soft music mingled with the merry cacophony of voices eagerly engaged in conversation within.

Delicious aromas of flavorful *biryanis* and succulent *kebabs* wafted through the air, along with the desserts that would as a perfect end to the meal. For the main course, there was a tomato-based chicken curry and a divine fish curry in mustard gravy.

Shiraj seemed a bit lost, and Afsana did her best to give him attention. He was not part of the bustling bridal party helping the bride get ready. But she reassured him that he was important regardless. After all, hadn't he footed the bill for this lavish event?

Razia's wedding was a bittersweet day for them both. She knew he was thrilled about his daughter's wedding, happy she had found the right groom, and overjoyed that her future looked bright. But they were also losing her. She was once that tiny baby girl he held in his arms. The wedding day marked the move of their daughter from her father's family into her groom's.

Afsana remembered her own wedding rituals—when she married Farzad, an ill-fated marriage destroyed by war. She and

Shiraj had not enjoyed the same beautiful celebration, her parents gone and his having outcast their son. No, the two of them had wed quickly and simply, without the support of family and friends, without the days-long celebrations. And yet, theirs was the marriage that lasted for decades. Her heart ached for Shiraj that he never enjoyed the thrill of being a groom at the center of all the outpouring of love and affection of family and friends. And her admiration for him grew even more, as she could see he did not resent it one bit. His focus was only on giving his daughter the best possible day.

With a shudder, she raised herself from her chair and went to the room where her daughter was dressed and waiting for the momentous occasion.

Razia donned a stunning golden saree and accessorized her look with chandelier earrings that not only matched her outfit but also made her look complete, adding an elegant touch to her ensemble. Her hair was styled to draw attention to her cheek bones. The sequined, transparent veil fastened on her head did not conceal her beauty, but only gave it the heightened charm of mystery. Her skin glowed from the pre-wedding ritual of *gaye holud*, where the ladies had put fresh turmeric paste on her. Her hands and feet were adorned with beautiful intricate designs of *mehendi*.

In no time, doubts began to sting Razia's heart, but it was impossible to stop the wedding now. The past few months came back to her vividly. She remembered Ayaan being brave, calm, and sorrowful. And there was that summer, that summer of her dreams, so far away now.

"Razia!"

She startled from her reverie. Somebody had called.

Her grief for not marrying the man she loved had lent a

deeper, darker hue to her eyes, and the sadness that shone in them seemed obvious to her.

"Razia! Aren't you coming, dear?" Her mother entered the room. "Oh, Razia. Look at you! You are absolutely beautiful in that gold color. It looks made just for you."

As her mother's eyes brimmed with happy tears, Razia's filled with tears of anguish. Today was the day she sealed a pact with another man, ending all chance of a future with Ayaan.

Another knock at the door had them both dabbing their eyes. "Come in," Razia said.

It was Auntie Nafisa.

Overjoyed to see Nafisa, she gave her a warm embrace as she came in, careful not to smudge her makeup or muss her hair.

"Oh, Razia, don't you look gorgeous. The most beautiful bride I've ever seen, my dear child! The man you marry will be a lucky man indeed," Auntie Nafisa rattled on. "You look as stunning as your mother did on her—"

Ammu shot a warning glance at Nafisa and shook her head.

Nafisa recovered quickly. "Razia, I must tell you something very important. I should have shared it with you when it first happened. My brother Nasir found me after all these years. And when I agreed to the reunion, he brought my son. I never expected to see him again and it was difficult for me to share this."

Ammu hugged Auntie. "I am so happy you have found him. I know the difficulties we endured are tangled up with motherhood for us. But we survived and we have beautiful children."

Razia watched the two most important women in her life console one another. When they dried each other's tears, both of them seemed refreshed and at ease in a way she hadn't seen them before.

"I hope it's okay, but I brought him with me to the wedding today. I am trying to spend as much time as I can with him while he is in town."

"Of course, Nafisa!" Ammu said. "We are thrilled to have him here. I cannot wait to meet him. Our two children under the same roof!"

Ammu embraced Nafisa and they both cried happily in each other's arms again. This time when they recovered, Ammu dried her eyes.

"Enough of that. Are you ready for your wedding?"

Razia took a deep breath and nodded.

Before she was led by her mother to be seated in a decorated room, Razia was guided through the admiring groups, with a smile here, a word there, the guests a lovely mosaic of color in all their finery. The women fussed over her, complimenting her outfit and dabbing at her make-up unnecessarily.

Suddenly, Razia spotted Ayaan amongst the guests. Her heart stopped. What was he doing at her wedding? She gave a little cry as she beckoned him to come nearer.

They were both silent and his face told her of the sorrow which his silence tried to conceal. After a vain effort to speak to him, she quickly wiped away tears that already welled up in her eyes, and with tenderness in her voice, she talked to him in as calm a manner as she could, so that no one would suspect they had met before and loved each other.

"What are you doing here, Ayaan?" she said nervously.

"I came with my mother," he said. "I must say it's a bit of a shock. I had no hope you would be my wife, Razia, but I wish you had told me."

"I am so sorry, Ayaan. I think some part of me didn't want to believe this would happen. I held on to hope—"

"Here comes my mother." He pointed to Nafisa.

"You are Nafisa's son?" Razia could not hide the shock. If only they had known. Perhaps they could have had a chance. Her parents knew Nafisa. They might have approved of this match.

Auntie Nafisa took Ayaan's hands into hers and brought him before Ammu and Abbu.

"This is Ayaan, my dear friends, my one and only son." Nafisa's eyes glistened with joy and happiness.

"Welcome, Ayaan! What a beautiful name and what a joy to have you among us! And that, too, on the day of our daughter's wedding," Ammu said.

"Yes, you are most welcome," Abbu agreed. "Your mother is like family to us, which means you are too."

"And have you met my daughter, Razia?" Ammu asked.

"I have met him, Ammu." Razia's whispered words caught her mother's attention.

"You know each other? You met before today?"

Ayaan nodded his head.

Ammu pierced her with a questioning look, but Razia only shook her head. She could not discuss this right now. Already she felt like an empty shell of herself and worried she might collapse. Why must fate taunt her so? Sending her true love to witness her marrying another man was the worst possible wedding gift the universe could give her.

Ammu seemed to sense something dire was transpiring within her daughter. She quickly covered, clasping Nafisa's arm. "Didn't I tell you that you'd find your son one day!"

Despite her cheerful disposition, Razia knew her mother well and recognized the undercurrent of interest in finding out more about Nafisa's son and how he knew her daughter. But she could hardly utter the questions she was burning to ask under the present circumstances. It was time for the wedding to begin.

Amidst all the merriment and excitement of the day, one thing was missing: the groom.

The clock was ticking away, well past the scheduled time of his arrival. The assembled guests grew impatient and started murmuring.

Afsana wrung her hands. "I had a feeling something was going to go wrong. Razia, my dear child—"

One of the guests touched her on the elbow and pointed

toward the door. A servant beckoned Afsana out of the room and informed her that a gentleman had arrived and was waiting in the parlor. He wished to speak with Shiraj.

A chill rattled Afsana's bones as she motioned for Shiraj to join her.

In the parlor, the stranger handed a sealed envelope to Shiraj, then departed.

Afsana watched anxiously as her husband read the letter and his face turned ashen.

"What has happened?" she whispered to her husband.

"It is from the groom's father. The wedding is canceled," Shiraj uttered in a tone of disbelief.

Afsana took the note from Shiraj and read the contents, unable to believe this was happening.

She sank into a chair. "What do we do now?" She rose and paced the floor, wringing her hands. "What will people say? What a mockery. Who has ever heard of a wedding ceremony where the groom didn't arrive?"

"It will be okay," Shiraj attempted to comfort her.

"Why should this happen to her? Razia is innocent. She does not deserve this. What reason do they give?"

Shiraj took the letter back. "He says they have objections to this marriage. He reminds us of their high social standing and that they are a well-known, respectable family. They will not allow their son to marry someone who they believe has an obscure past."

Afsana thought she might be sick. When he spoke again, his voice was strange and choked, and his words sent a rippling chill through Afsana's body.

"He says the information came to them from their trusted family friend, Farzad Mansour," Shiraj said. "How could he do this? Here I worried he would arrive uninvited and cause a scene. But no, he has struck deeply this time."

"I cannot believe this. He cares a great deal about Razia. He even gave her glass bangles to wear on this, her wedding day."

"No father in his right mind would jeopardize his daughter's wedding. He cannot possibly care about her. I've told you all along he was bad news."

At that moment, she wished the earth would open up and swallow her. Afsana stood still, chewing on her lip, shifting her glance around the room, avoiding eye contact. She tried to change the subject. "We should go back out and comfort Razia. The poor girl is probably—"

"Afsana, what does he mean when he refers to Razia's 'obscure past'?"

She twisted her hands together. "I have done an awful thing, Shiraj. When you found me in the refugee camp, you assumed the child I carried was fathered by Farzad. I did not correct you then. I have been trying to find a way to tell you the truth, but it is so difficult."

"What are you saying?" His voice, low and quiet, scared her.

Tears filled her eyes. "I was not pregnant when I was taken captive during the war. In the barracks, the men—" She stopped, afraid she would vomit if she spoke the truth. But it was there, hanging in the air like the stench of smoldering rubbish. Not only was her daughter's future ruined, but hers was as well. Shiraj would be justified in throwing her out, divorcing her for deceiving him. Farzad had sealed her fate, doomed them both to a life of solitude. His revenge cut her to the quick.

Shiraj's eyes glazed over, and he turned away. "All those nightmares. All that suffering—"

"Please, Shiraj! You're all she knows. You are her father. You bathed her and fed her and tucked her in and held her when she cried. Do what you wish to me, throw me out on the streets. But do not let our daughter suffer because I made a mistake."

He stood still, silent.

Tears streaked her face. "I try not to think about it, Shiraj. The time I spent in the camp . . . I was helpless. They tortured me for information about Farzad. I had nothing to give them, but they didn't believe me. Or perhaps they simply enjoyed hurting me. Eventually, they tired of that and turned to . . . another form of torture. Day after day, night after night—" She gagged, the memory of the pain and shame, the repeated violation—

"Enough," Shiraj said, and his voice choked.

Shocked, Afsana turned to look at him and discovered tears in his eyes.

"I cannot bear the thought of my Afsana brutalized in such a way. You are a *birangona*, a war heroine, just as if you had marched into battle." He opened his arms and welcomed her in a tight embrace. He rubbed his hands up and down her back and murmured soft words of comfort for wounds long ago inflicted that had never healed.

"Oh, Shiraj." She choked back tears that stung her eyes. "I have wronged you once again. Will you ever forgive me?"

"Nothing to forgive. Do not apologize for something over which you had no control. We will never speak of this again. Now, dry your eyes. Our daughter is waiting."

～

Razia stood amidst her wedding guests, embarrassed and bewildered. Mixed emotions swirled through her. After all, she had not wanted to marry this man anyway. But being jilted stung her ego.

When her mother and father returned, she looked eagerly for answers. Ammu had clearly been crying but was smiling now and more relaxed than she had appeared in days. Abbu held Ammu's hand and beamed upon her with pride. Then he addressed the assembled guests.

"We have had a change of plans," he announced. "After a last-minute message from the groom's family, we have decided to retract our approval of this match. Our daughter deserves better."

"Abbu?" she asked.

He held out an arm to her and hugged her close, whispering, "And perhaps this time, you shall marry for love, yes?"

Nafisa joined them. "What has happened?"

"We learned some new information about the intended groom," Shiraj told her. "He is not the man we thought he was. And his family not nearly as upstanding as we believed."

Razia could not believe what she was hearing. But both parents seemed so happy, so relieved, that she dared not utter a word.

"Everyone, please," Shiraj called. "Let us enjoy all the food! Today is a good day."

"If I could please say something first?"

They all turned. Razia's heart skipped a beat at the sound of that voice.

Ayaan approached, his dark eyes fastened upon her as she stared back from behind her bridal veil.

"There are a few words I wish to say if you would permit me, sir and ma'am."

Auntie Nafisa's brow furrowed. "Ayaan? What is this?"

"Razia and I met at school, and we fell in love. I know this will seem sudden, and I know I don't have much yet, but I will treat her as the jewel she is and treasure her all her life. If I may be so bold."

Abbu, a bemused smile about his lips, nodded.

Ayaan turned to her and took her hand in his. "Will you marry me, Razia?"

The sound of his voice strengthened her and lifted her spirits. She raised her head and looked to her parents. Both of them smiled and nodded their consent.

"Yes, Ayaan! Yes!"

There was a sudden stillness, and then silence broke into joyful shouts.

"We are having a wedding today after all!" Ammu cried.

Soft silk sarees rustled again, voices chattered, little peals of laughter broke forth. And the assembled guests fell into their places in the wedding pomp, eager to join in the renewal of the wedding ceremonies.

The servant appeared once again, opening the door to an unseen visitor.

"Now what could this be?" Ammu asked.

Nasir appeared in the doorway. "Sorry I'm late. Have I missed it?"

"You are just in time to see Ayaan wed!" Auntie Nafisa laughed.

Nasir looked back and forth between Razia and Ayaan then broke into laughter too. "Marvelous!" he said as he took a seat next to Auntie Nafisa.

Razia reached for Ayaan's hand and stepped forward, her heart singing with joy.

~

As the wedding ceremony commenced, Afsana stood beside her husband and her best friend Nafisa, marveling at the unexpected turn of events. Razia beamed in delight. Her daughter was marrying her best friend's son, a source of joy springing from unbearable pain.

"Don't cry, my dears," Shiraj said. "This is a happy day."

Afsana squeezed his hand. "And these are happy tears. It has always been a source of pain to me that I kept a secret from you. I feel today as though the last black cloud has been swept away by a refreshing breeze."

Something improbable had occurred on this blissful night. And it was nearly impossible to believe that it had unfolded to such a happy conclusion. Watching the ceremony, and the sheer joy on Razia's face, Afsana began believing in fairy tales.

Afsana reached for Nafisa and gave her hand to her friend in silence. Life had stopped being beautiful for them. They had lived through inhuman horrors, but worse, they had been shunned, blamed for things which could not be otherwise. And, they had blamed themselves for all the evil that had befallen them.

The scars of their war might never fully fade. Some days, they were open wounds, festering in secrecy. They would haunt them as long as they lived. The mind learned to adapt, to move on. But the pain was never gone. Sometimes it shrank to the size of a pinprick, but always it remained, reminding them that they survived, that they were strong enough to fight through. And that was real strength. Perhaps Shiraj's understanding and forgiveness would allow her to forgive herself.

In this moment, she had every reason to be happy.

She squeezed Nafisa's hand. Together they would shoulder the pain and the guilt. Together they could strive for self-forgiveness and self-compassion. They were *birangona*, their fates darkened by great sorrows but not without rewards. After the darkness, they had finally found their light.

From the Author

The novel *My War, My Child* gives voice to life beyond war and its onward challenges.

War often most impacts women and children. The novel deals with the prevalent understanding that wartime violence against women is engulfed in silence, since the most shameful consequence of conflict comes out into the open. It leaves unwanted children who serve as constant reminders of the worst day of their mothers' lives. They were not only wounded physically and emotionally; they also have been shunned and condemned by their families.

Children of war can't change what happened. Their origins reveal lasting legacies of conflict, including traumas, birth family separations, stigmatization, and integration challenges.

But these innocent victims can lead normal lives, given the opportunity. With love and acceptance, they can change their perceptions of what happened and learn to reconstruct their lives. How? The story shows that, in a safe environment, they can revisit their traumas and renounce false guilt or shame.

With non-judgmental transparency, they are able to gain a new perspective, enabling them to move forward with a new appreciation of themselves, for others, and the world around them.

Instead of helpless defeat, they can acquire a new strength of successful survivor, poised to grow beyond their pain and help others still trapped by their own sense of loss.

About the Author

Bharati Sen was born in Yangon, Myanmar and spent much of her childhood growing up in South Asia in West Bengal. She completed a Master's degree in International Relations and discovered a passion for writing about social disparities and cultural differences. Her debut award-winning book, *On the Banks of River Sarayu*, is a compilation of nineteen stories reflecting the lives of ordinary South Asian women within bittersweet tales. The book was awarded finalist in the Women's Issues category of the 2020 International Book Awards as well as the 2020 finalist for the MiPA Midwest Book Award in the category of Short Stories. Bharati currently lives in Tulsa, Oklahoma with her husband and two sons.

f g a

Also by Bharati Sen

On the Banks of River Sarayu

More by Admission Press

Looking for your next great read?
Visit www.admissionpress.com

Made in the USA
Coppell, TX
24 March 2024

30479187R00121